Marvin and His Cow Dogs

True Stories by
Marvin Pierce

Published by
Marvin Pierce
Newberg, OR
www.PiercesCowDogs.com

ISBN: 978-1-4675-3246-4

Printed in the United States of America

Disclaimer

These stories are told to the best of my memory. Specific information may have been changed, such as names, places and dates in order to preserve individual privacy and so no one can come back and tell me I got it all wrong!

Acknowledgments

I would like to dedicate this book of short stories to all the people, horses and cow dogs that made this possible. This especially includes my lovely wife Jodi for putting up with me and my dogs, my stepdaughter Laura for all the times she caught my horses, brushed them and saddled them for me and even loaded them while I got my gear ready; and my stepson Jason who has helped me catch many of the cattle that are in these stories.

I also want to acknowledge in memory my horses Buddy and Roany, may they find green pastures always. I owe a lot to my Quarter Horse Badger who has been a reliable cow horse through all sorts of difficult conditions.

Then there are the dogs. I'll always fondly remember my first Border Collie Jake who put up with me and taught me so much about training cow dogs. And of course my cattle gathering experience would never have gone so well in those early years without my first Hangin' Tree Cowdog Sport and Cattle Master Dog Chic. For eleven years Sport helped me gather some of the toughest cattle around. He was the coolest dog ever. Sport passed away January 2011 from heart failure. My Cattle Master Dog Chic was by far the best female cow dog I ever owned. Sadly Chic died when a bull she was working broke her neck. I will miss them both.

And many thanks go to all the people who let me catch their cattle, work my dogs on their cattle and trusted me to help them solve their cattle problems. That also goes for all the people, on horseback and on foot who helped me and my dogs catch cattle. Special thanks go to Mike and Mandy Marriot of Marriot's Performance Horses for helping me train my cattle-gathering horses. Also Wiley and Stacey Henry of Lone Star Arena for all the times they've called me to gather cattle or catch cattle. I'd also like to acknowledge Adrienne of Equine Online Design for reworking the stories and making me sound sensible.

I have changed some of the names throughout this story, nothing personal, just wanted to keep anonymity for those folks I thought might appreciate it.

I'm sure there are folks I'm forgetting as the list of people who helped me with this book or who made these stories possible is long. Just know that when I see you I'll know who you are and I'll thank you for all you've done.

Contents

Introduction

I've written this book of short stories in an attempt to capture the humor and excitement I've experienced with my work gathering cattle. The success I've had with cattle has only come about because of the amazing cow dogs I've raised and trained and the fine horses that packed me along through all sorts of tough situations.

The breed of dog I use for most of my cattle work is called a "Hangin' Tree Cowdog". This breed came about in the mid 1980s and is a cross between the Border Collie, Kelpie, Catahoula and Australian shepherd. I also use another breed of dog called a Cattle Master which is a mix of Border Collie, Kelpie and American Bull Dog. I like to cross these two breed types, the "Hangin' Tree Cowdog" and the Cattle Master, and have had some great dogs from the mix. One of the goals of raising dogs is to try and reproduce as good a dog as what you already have.

In some of my stories it may sound like my dogs and I are pretty rough on the cattle. In all the years I've been working dogs on cattle I've never had to call a vet to come doctor an animal I caught with my dogs. What people don't understand about cow dogs is that it's not always about my dogs fighting and chewing on cattle; it's about respect and getting the cattle to move without my dogs fighting them. That's where training and working the dogs and cattle together comes in. That is the goal with my dogs. If the bulls or cows get mad enough and they don't have that foundation of respect for the dogs then they'll charge the dogs, possibly hurt the horse and rider and run down any fence in their way. Learning respect is what keeps that from happening.

It's important to note that this book doesn't have all the hundreds of stories about the times I go gather cattle and they just go quietly into the corrals because that would be a rather boring book. The stories in this book are about the cattle that people have been chasing for awhile with no success. Some of these failed attempts have involved 6 or 8 people on horses with no luck. It usually is only after hours or days of struggle that a cattle owner will finally decide to call me because they've heard of me and my dogs, they're tired of wasting their time and money, they can see the effects of the stress on their cattle and they just want their cattle caught before they're hurt and more property is damaged!

Using my dogs on cattle makes them gentler because my methods don't involve chasing them. The dogs I use are tough enough to stop the cattle from running. Once the cattle are stopped it's a lot easier for the dogs to control their movements following my commands.

I also gather a lot of cattle for folks that I have already "dog-broke" and sometimes I don't even have to take a horse to pen them. I usually only take one dog because those cattle have been trained to respond to my dogs and have learned to have respect for them. In these times there's not a cow that even gets bit while being penned up.

There are also times when I show up to gather cattle and the first thing the owners will tell me is how their cows are going to try and kill my dogs because they already ran their dogs out of the field. So I have to have really tough and well trained dogs to teach these cows that my dogs are the boss. Once that happens, gathering them up becomes easier!

A very important trait or characteristic I require in my cattle dogs is they have to be good around people. My kids have always been able to play with our working dogs. A lot of people say their working dogs can't be family pets. I won't own a dog like that; I want my kids and my grandkids to be able to play with my dogs.

I often have people ask me why I use the "Hangin' Tree Cowdog" and Cattle Master breeds instead of Border Collies or Heelers. I feel Heelers are bred to push cattle. I want my dogs to stop cattle. I have owned several Border Collies over the years and they're a great dog. They just don't quite do the kind of rigorous cattle work that I need done.

I have done a lot of things that people say I'm crazy for even trying. I have been working dogs for a long time now and I feel I have tried about everything you probably shouldn't try to do with a dog. But, I've also caught a whole lot of cows that I was told couldn't be caught and that's only because of my awesome dogs.

Working Cattle Terminology

Here are a number of terms used by Marvin and others when training and working with cow dogs.

Head Box: A small enclosed pen where a horseback rider waits before running out into an arena to rope a steer by the horns. The head box is used in team roping rodeo events

Dally: To wind the lasso rope around the horn of a western saddle after roping stock

Balled up, Bayed up or Bay 'em: When the dogs go out and stop the cattle then make them stay where they're at, clumped together, until a person shows up to give them more instruction

Honda: A knot commonly used in a lasso rope. Its round shape, especially when tied in stiff rope, helps it slide freely along the rope it's tied around

Limousin Cattle: A heavily muscled breed of cattle originating from France

Stripping Chute: Where you take roping steers after you rope them to take your rope off

Sort 3 out of 6: When you take some of the cattle and leave some behind

Leave the country: Means the cattle are going to run off.

Caught up: Same as bayed up; stopping the cattle and holding them in a circle until a person arrives

Pen: Same as a corral; a place to hold cattle

Cow-calf pairs: A momma cow and her baby

Corral: A place to hold cattle to be sorted or loaded into a trailer.

Brushing up: Same as baying up, only the dogs get the cattle stopped in the brush

Blowing: Blowing air out of the nostrils forcibly; for cattle and horses

Snorting: When they're mad and trumpeting air out their nostrils; for cattle and horses

Loping: A three beat running gait of a horse that is fast in speed

Trot: Two beat gait of a horse where the diagonal pairs of legs work at the same time; a medium speed gait

Panels: Metal pre-fab fence pieces, usually 8 – 12 feet sections that you use to build a corral or a chute for cattle

Bawling: A vocal sound cattle make when they are distressed, i.e. when a baby is missing or they're fighting coyotes, dogs, etc....

Look back: Command for the dog to look back in the opposite direction and go get stray stock

Cinch: Part of a western saddle that goes under the belly of a horse and keeps the saddle secured down on the horse's back

Choked down: Tighten the lasso rope up a little around the stock's neck so that they settle down and quite fighting

Leave 'em: Command for a dog to leave the stock they are working on

Bring 'em: Command for a dog to bring the stock to the person who gave the command

Watch him: Command for a dog to watch the stock so they don't move

Walk up: Command for a dog to walk toward the stock

Marvin and
His Cow Dogs

Chapter 1
A Good Pet and Working Dog Too!

I talk to people a lot about working dogs and quite often what I hear is you shouldn't try to make a pet out of your working cow dog because it'll mess up their ability to be a great cow dog. I happen to disagree with this. Some of the excellent working cow dogs I've had slept by my bed or even in my lap if I let them. They were great working dogs and wonderful family dogs too.

When it comes to dogs, I'm not a person who will pet and love on my dogs all the time but that doesn't mean I don't care about them. I treat my dogs well. If they need a vet they get one. They are wormed when they should be, have a dry bed to sleep on and nice, clean kennel runs. My Hangin' Tree Cowdog, Sport, would lay by my feet and be as happy as a dog can be and let me pet on him anytime I wanted. But he didn't bug me to pet on him and that's what I especially liked about that dog. Don't get me wrong, I think it's a great thing if people want to pet on their dogs all the time; it's just not something I do.

I sold a nice cattle dog a while back because she really wanted to be loved and petted when she wasn't working and she wasn't getting enough of that from me. I thought she'd be happier with someone who had the time and inclination to give her the petting and loving attention she wanted.

I believe one of the things people don't understand about a cattle dog is that if they're from the bloodlines of great working dogs then they're going to "live to work". If they're going to be a good companion and a good working dog, then besides coming from good bloodlines, you're also going to have to spend a lot of time with them to get them where they will do whatever you tell them, when you tell them.

My dog, Sport, was my buddy, traveling companion and family dog but he also "lived" to work cattle! Sport passed away but he will always be remembered as one of my greatest working cow dogs as well as one of my best family dogs.

I also owned a Border Collie many years ago who was an awesome dog. My livestock and I were the only things that dog truly cared about. He wouldn't work for anyone but me, no exceptions. He would work at anything or on anything I asked him to. If I let him loose, he would gather stock and put them in my roping arena or at the gate and hold them till I found him. It didn't matter if it was five minutes or five hours, he would hold the stock and wait for me. But he was an "all-work" dog and none of the other stuff mattered to him.

What I want people to understand is that a cattle dog is not for everyone but they can make great pets. They need exercise and a lot of it, especially when they're young. I have seen my wife, Jodi, play ball with her dog Tren in our living room when we're watching TV. This dog is so amazing because Jodi can throw Tren's ball anywhere in the living room, any distance, and she will get it time and time again without breaking a thing and is about the happiest dog alive going after that ball!

Now that Tren is older and her youthful exuberance has simmered a bit she doesn't need the ball thrown for her as much. The thing is, when Tren was younger and needed that exercise all the time, she got it even though sometimes it had to be in the house because of weather or on account of it being later at night. Jodi taught her to be careful and not break anything. It just goes to show, you can have a working dog that's also a great pet!

I owned a Cattle Master female who sadly passed away at a young age but she was the most extraordinary female dog I ever owned as well as one of the toughest. She could work the biggest, meanest bull in the field in the morning than later that day play a gentle game of fetch with my little granddaughter. She was the kind of dog that would curl up and go to sleep in my lap if I let her!

So my thoughts are, if you want both a good pet and a good working cow dog, find one from the right parents, train it well, treat it kindly and give it lots of exercise. By doing this I believe you can develop both qualities, working cow dog and family pet, in the same dog.

Chapter 2
Breeds Of Cow Dogs I Have Owned

When I first started working cattle with dogs I used a Border Collie but I wasn't really happy with that breed choice. I feel their hair is too long and they get too hot. They are also too intense. They can spend the whole day just staring at livestock!

Later on I decided to try a different breed of dog. That's when I found out about the Hangin' Tree Cowdog. The Hangin' Tree Cowdog is bred from Border Collie, Kelpie, Catahoula Leopard Dog and Australian Shepherd. They are a registered breed and Gary Erickson from Oklahoma is the man who developed the breed standard. The criteria he came up with for the breed, and what's needed for registration, declare they have to be short-haired, bob-tailed and have a registered mom and dad. One of the things he did in developing this breed was to make sure he cut (or docked) their tales. That way brush and cactus wouldn't get stuck in their tails and cause problems or injuries while working. A wagging tail full of cactus can do a lot of damage to a dog's sides!

When you breed registered Hangin' Tree Cowdog parents you get appendix papers on the pups. To register that pup you have to send pictures or a video of the dog biting both the head and heels of cattle. Two viewers on the board of directors' watch your video or examine your pictures and decide if the dog can be registered.

The reason I went with the Hangin' Tree Cowdog is their reputation for being tough, hardy, a strong "head" dog (that's one that will work the front of the cow as much as the back of the cow), and a solid temperament. If you get your dog from registered parents who are known for their cattle work then you have a chance of having a good working dog with all those characteristics.

I tried the Catahoula Leopard dogs but they're pretty stubborn and hard-headed. They're harder to train and in my opinion not as good of a family dog as the Hangin' Tree Cowdog.

I fooled with the Kelpie breed back in the day and I didn't like those very much either. However, I have ended up working with them again. I have three or four Kelpies that I use and I really like them.

In the end I believe the breed of dog someone chooses just comes down to what is going to work the best for that person and what that person needs the dog to do.

I like to cross my Hangin' Tree Cowdogs with another favorite breed of mine called the Cattle Master. They are a mix of Border Collie, Kelpie and American Bull Dog. They're a real nice dog; a lot of bite to them, good herding instincts and they're super tough and short-haired. I have been very happy with the ones I've owned.

So in a nutshell, those are the breeds of dogs I've used. My favorites are the ones I've crossed using the Hangin' Tree Cowdog as the stud bred with a female Cattle Master. One of the best dogs I have is from that cross. His name is Tyson and I've been real happy with the way he's turning out. I hope I end up with a lot more like him someday!

Chapter 3
Are You Really Going To Keep
Your Cows Forever

Years ago I used to buy cows and calves from people who could no longer take care of them. Usually these folks bought the cattle thinking they would keep them for a long time, maybe breed them some, but quickly found out they couldn't handle them. Mostly it's because the cattle get out of control and are a bit wild, they're rough and break through fences or they're constantly getting out of good situations and into bad ones. The day finally comes when the owners decide they want to get rid of their cattle but they don't have any way to get them into a trailer and they don't even have any corrals to bring the cattle into so someone can get them into a trailer!

One day I saw an ad in the paper that read *'Three cows and a calf, cheap; can't load them!'* I thought this sounded like some fun work for me and my dogs and maybe a good deal on some cows as well!

I told my wife Jodi that I was going to call these people about the calf and cows they had for sale and make a good deal on them. I explained to her, "The people who own them can't get them in their trailer because they don't have any corrals. They just want them gone." Jodi just shook her head. I think she knew my ulterior motive of wanting to work my dogs. "I'm going to go get them. I'm taking Jake, Sport, and Cross with me."

"Really?" she asked in that rolling-her-eyes kind of way, like she can't believe I'm actually going to use this situation for a little dog training! "Well I'm coming with you!" she said and added, "And the kids too." Although she might not always admit it, Jodi liked the action of dogs working unruly cattle.

I didn't have any idea what I was getting myself into. I just knew this lady couldn't get her cows in a trailer and she didn't have a corral. So Jodi, our kids Jason and Laura, and the dogs piled into the truck with me and we all drove over to this lady's place to work…uh buy some cows.

When we arrived at her place I noticed she had this pretty little three-board fence all painted white surrounding about a half acre of pasture where she kept the cows. I was beginning to think this might be more challenging than I thought because the cows could easily tear up that pretty little fence, especially if they felt a little dog pressure on them!

After I introduced myself and my family, I asked the lady, "Have your cows ever been worked with dogs before?"

"Nope, never!" She told me. "But, they will follow a feed bucket sometimes."

"Well let's see if they'll follow a feed bucket into my trailer." We tried it and of course they weren't going to have anything to do with that trailer. After a few more failed attempts with the grain I stated, "Well…the only choice I see is to use my dogs."

"Okay" she said then continued "Those cows are yours now. Do what you want. But I want to keep the big one." At that time all three of my dogs were working really well and they listened to me perfectly so I felt we were going to be able to accomplish this task.

"The first thing I'm going to do is let the dogs ball them up in the middle of this little pen here and teach them not to run off." The lady was plenty agreeable to my plan.

Her pen happened to go around the barn just a bit and I couldn't see around that corner. I had my trailer backed up to the pen's gate which was open, along with my trailer gate, and ready for those cows to run into my trailer. Mind you, I was still new at this cattle gathering stuff. I turned my dogs loose and those cows immediately shot around to the back side of the barn, just out of my view. I waited for them to reappear with the dogs on their tail but they didn't come back! I could hear the dogs barking but it was sounding a bit farther off than just around the corner. The lady ran around to the side of the barn and shouted, "Oh my gosh! Somebody left the back gate open behind the barn." I ran out of the pen and sure enough, the back gate was left open.

Like I said, I was new enough at this that I didn't think of walking the perimeter of that pen to make sure all the gates were closed before I started rounding up the cows.

At this point I could still hear the dogs barking and the cows bawling but I couldn't see them yet. I could tell the dogs had them stopped somewhere when all of a sudden this lady yelled, "Oh my God! They're out in my parking lot. They aren't even in my field!" She was starting to get a bit hysterical. "What are we going to do now?"

"I'm not sure," I said. What I really wanted was for her to calm down a little. "How about if we all just stay back for a sec. The dogs have them bayed up and they're not moving so we're good for now." I'm standing there thinking about what to do because I don't want these cows running loose in the countryside or even in the parking lot! I don't even have a horse with me in case I had to chase them.

"Alright everybody, let's all just stand back!" An idea had come to me. "They came out this gate and we'll get them back in." I carefully walked over to where my dogs had the cows stopped, which wasn't too far off thankfully. I instructed my dogs to get on the back side of the cows and lay down. The cows started wandering towards the gate so I had my dogs get up and slowly creep forward, guiding them toward me and the gate. The lady started talking but I had to quickly interrupt her, "Please don't say anything. Everybody just be calm and don't say a word till we get them in the corral." Everybody practically held their breath! The dogs slowly walked those cows up to the corral until they were all finally in and I could run over and shut the gate.

The lady said, "My gosh, that was so neat!"

"It'll be neater when they're in my trailer." I joked with her. I got the dogs to circle around the cows and any time a cow tried to take off I sent one of the dogs to get ahead and chew on it a little. Like I said, I had some nice dogs who listened really well to whatever I told them to do!

All the dogs were working together like they knew things were serious. It took about ten minutes of working these cows before they were all in the trailer and I was feeling relieved. Then the lady reminded me, "Marvin, did you forget? I want to keep that one." She's pointing to the biggest cow in the trailer who happens to be huddled right in the middle of all of them.

Well, I had forgotten. I exclaimed, "Well, guess I'll just keep moving them around in the trailer till we get that big one by the slider door near the back then I'll kick him out."

I made the dogs leave the corral and go lie down so they could have a rest. Then my wife, the kids, and I hung on the sides of the trailer trying to shoo this cow over to the side door. It was kind of like playing musical chairs! It took us a few minutes but we finally got that cow lined up by the door. I slid the door open, the cow shot out real fast and just as quickly I slid that door shut again.

When everyone had the cows they were supposed to have, this lady said to me, "That is just so impressive what you and your dogs did. I've never seen anything like that."

"It's always nice when it works out but just remember, it doesn't always work out!" I told her. We got the trailer gate secured and everything and everyone loaded up; dogs, gear, people. Then we took off towards home…with three new cows! That was a good day for me and my dogs.

Chapter 4
Why I Got Into Working Cow Dogs
1998

It was about 1998 when I started team roping. Every time I went roping at one of the big arenas in the area, there would be people out there trying to catch the roping steers. They would be chasing them around with horses and a lot of times they had to wait until three or four people got there to help catch those steers. I never once gave it any mind that gathering up those roping steers could be done any differently. I was just glad I wasn't the one running around after those steers.

Then my wife and I bought some steers to keep at our house so we and the kids could practice a little team roping. At this time I had a lot of brush behind my arena. My steers were always running off and hiding in the brush and we had to go in on foot to catch them since we couldn't get the horses back there. Sometimes it would be two hours later by the time we got them caught. By then nobody wanted to rope anymore because we were all too tired. It got to the point where catching these steers on foot was not going to work for our team roping practices, especially since I was the one on foot now!

So I started looking for a cow dog. I'd never even seen a cow dog work. I got a copy of a *'Western Horseman'* magazine and read about Gary Erickson who was raising "Hangin' Tree Cowdogs." I decided what I needed was a cow dog. I really wanted to get a Hangin' Tree Cowdog but the problem was I lived in Oregon and the only place these dogs could be found back then was in Oklahoma. So instead of making the trip out there I ended up buying a Border Collie named Jake from a guy I worked with.

I spent a lot of time training Jake. At first I had to keep him on a rope because I couldn't turn him loose without him running off. After I trained him not to run off I discovered he had a heck of a bite to him. He'd latch on to a cow and just wouldn't let go. I wanted to use Jake to help get my cattle into the roping arena but we still had some things to work out. It was then that I started looking at Gary's information again and decided to call him up and talk a bit about dog training. I ended up buying four or five cow dog training videos from him and used those to help train Jake, who ended up being a super cow dog.

Things were going well with Jake's training and his cow work. Soon Jake and I started catching cows for local people. That was okay for a while but I soon realized that Jake wasn't going to work out for me for several reasons, a couple being that his hair was too long and he got too hot. That was a problem since a lot of our cow work was during the summer and often in hot weather. Although he was a great dog, he just wasn't quite what I needed for the kind of cattle work I was getting into.

So in the end I flew out to Oklahoma to buy a Hangin' Tree Cowdog after all! And that's how I got into working cow dogs!

Chapter 5
The Things I Can Get Myself Into
1999

One hot day in 1999 I got a phone call from a guy named Ken. He started off by saying he was told I hauled livestock for people. I said I do sometimes, depending on what needs hauling. He told me he had bought a whole herd of goats and needed them hauled to the sale barn. We talked for awhile about it and I asked him if he had a stock dog. He informed me that he had a great stock dog but we wouldn't even need any dogs because the goats would be penned up when we got there.

I was kind of new at gathering stock but I knew enough to know you didn't haul stock without a stock dog so I decided to take my Border Collie Jake along. Ken told me he had about two loads apiece for each of us and the round trip to the sale barn was about 140 miles. It sounded like it was going to be a long day; that's if everything went well!

I met Ken at a restaurant and we had a bite of lunch before we got started. During lunch I asked him about his great dog and he told me he left him home. It was 101 degrees outside that day and too hot for his dog!

After our meal we drove out to the farm to get Ken's herd of goats. When we got out of our trucks I could see some pens but there were no goats in them! I started looking around and there were a lot of goats out in the fields and rolling hills! I asked Ken what the deal was and he said he was told they would be in the pens. By this time the owner walked over from his house and told us he wasn't sure when we were going to be there so he left the goats out because it was so hot. He said it wouldn't be a problem getting them in.

We walked out in the field to get the goats and realized after several hot tries they were having nothing to do with going into the pen. We were all sweaty and dusty by then and I told Ken I was not chasing anymore goats.

Ken and the other guy tried for a few more minutes while I watched from my truck with my good dog Jake sitting next to me.

After a while they walked to my truck and asked if I would gather the goats for them with my dog. I said I would but wouldn't be responsible for any goat that didn't cooperate with my dog. I told them Jake was a cow dog, not a goat dog, and he might get a little rough with those goats! Ken and the other guy were so hot and tired they didn't care.

I sent Jake out and he was awesome! He rounded up what I thought were all the goats and herded them into the pen but the owner hollered at me and said there were a few more over the next little hill. I told Jake to "Look back" and he went back over that hill and brought the last of the goats to the pen. We loaded both trailers with goats and drove them to the sale barn.

When we got back we loaded the second, and last, batch of goats. The man who had sold the goats to Ken told him to take the llamas too – all three of them. Well those lamas did not want to go into the trailer! The owner put halters on them and tried to lead them into Ken's trailer but they wouldn't budge. Ken and the owner pulled and pushed and sweated a whole lot before they finally asked me to help. I laughed at them and said to get those llamas headed into the trailer and watch out because I was going to have Jake bite their heels! Ken said, "No way Marvin! Those llamas will kill Jake." I assured Ken that wasn't going to happen and again asked everyone to stand back. I gave Jake the command to "Bite" and he did! Those llamas jumped into that trailer and we were done!

That was many years ago but I still get in those kinds of predicaments to this day; but I sure do enjoy them. I get to work my dogs in some challenging and unique situations and some darn funny ones too!

Chapter 6
Whose Cows Are Whose?
1999

Our landlord used to keep her cows with my cows on the property we leased from her. I owned a Border Collie at that time named Jake. Our landlady was adamant that I DID NOT work her cows with my dogs. I think she was afraid that my dogs might hurt them. Fortunately there was only one mama cow and two calves.

I figured I had better start teaching Jake how to go into the herd of cattle, leave her three and bring mine! No one believed I could do this. In fact, everybody thought it was pretty darn funny at the time.

I put all the cattle in my arena one day and started working Jake. Every time he went for one of her cows I told him to "Leave 'em", which is the command I use when I don't want my dogs to bring me an animal. I would make him get away from her cows and then I would have him bring my cattle to me.

This went on for about two weeks. Every day when I got home from work I went to my arena and worked Jake with all the cattle. I taught him that her three could not be worked. It was kind of neat to watch him as he learned to do this!

My cattle were usually roping steers with horns but her cows didn't have horns. I decided I was going to take the next step in Jake's training. I was going to get a cow without horns and see if Jake would understand that he could work that one if I told him to.

I ended up getting a cow without horns, put it in with the herd, and then got Jake working all the cattle. It didn't take too much time for me to teach him that he could bring that hornless cow in with mine but he still had to leave my landlady's three.

This went on for another three or four weeks. I then decided I was going to try it out in the big field. To me a big field is about 20 or 30 acres. I put all the cattle out in that big field and started working Jake. It was no problem for him; he left the landlady's three cows alone and still brought my cow without the horns in along with my other cattle.

I decided to go a little further. I got a cow that was the same color as hers and also didn't have horns and put it out with Jake and taught him to bring it in along with my cattle. I was curious to see if he would learn that too! In a couple of weeks he knew the difference between my cows and the landlady's cows.

About that time I decided to sell Jake. I had just started working with my new dog, Hangin' Tree Sport and teaching him the same thing. At one time I had him out with 20 head of cattle. I had cattle with and without horns, all kinds and colors and all different sizes! Sport would go out and gather up all my cattle but he would leave the landlady's cows alone!

The landlady's three cows were unruly, ornery and hard to work. Luckily I didn't have to work them. We just left them alone. I could send my dog out to get my cows and not even see her cows. Sport would bring back my cattle and leave her three out in the field. This continued to be the situation for a least a year or two. Then one day the landlady decided I could work her cows!

Man, it took me a while to convince Sport he could work those cows. Finally I was able to get him to bring them in along with all of mine. The one good thing about all that hard work I put into training Sport was if we were working cattle and I told him to leave something, he would leave it. It didn't matter if it was a steer, bull, cow, or calf. He learned that sometimes I didn't want him to bring a particular cow but I did want him to bring the rest of the herd. At that time I also taught him to "Look back" and that meant to go back and get what he had left or pick up stragglers. If I told him to leave a cow and I went off across the field two or three hundred feet then wanted him to go back and get that cow, I just told him "Look back" and he would go get the stock and bring it to me!

It's amazing what a cow dog can learn to do with a lot of patience, some hard work and changing instructions!

Chapter 7
The Day My Steer Ran Over My Wife
Winter 2000

Some friends of mine have a big indoor arena and I use it on a regular basis to work my dogs on cattle. One day I was planning to take some young dogs and a bunch of calves over to the arena. I needed to get those young dogs started. Usually while I'm there I'll let my wife and a few friends do some cutting on the calves with their horses.

Getting ready to head out to the arena with the dogs, calves, horses and my wife is always an ordeal to pull off. Especially in winter because we live near Portland, Oregon and it rains a lot! First I have to hook the trailer up and park it in such a way that I can load the cattle. This can be difficult when the ground is muddy. Then I have to get the dogs out and put their collars on. And finally the dogs and I have to head off into the rain and mud to find my calves that always seem to be as far from the house as they can get. Luckily for me that's only about 4 hundred yards.

On this particular wet and muddy day I had already sent my dogs Sport and Chic to get the calves and bring them in. They ended up meeting me with the herd about half way out so I turned and started walking back to the barn lot. Sport and Chic brought the calves along behind me. When we got to the barn lot it was raining like crazy so I was in a big hurry. And of course everyone knows when you're in a hurry nothing goes right!

Once we got the calves in the corral I sorted out the ones I wanted to take with us. At the time we had this one calf we called DQ who liked running up to my wife. She figured it was because she was always nice to him. But I felt it was because DQ was just plain weird – he'd come running up to you whenever he saw a dog. I was thinking how I really didn't want to take this calf but wouldn't you know, he ran right up into the trailer. In the meantime I had the dogs help me sort out ones that I wanted to take along. By that time I was pretty wet so I decide what the heck; I'd just take DQ, no harm in it. I still remember this day eight years later and how that ended up being such a bad idea! My wife reminds me about it quite often too!

When the calves were finally loaded I backed the truck and trailer in the horse barn so we could load the horses. My wife and I saddled our horses and loaded them up. I decided to take one of my young dogs, Hidden Canyon Cross, so I put him in a dog crate in the truck bed next to the others. When all that was done I finally went to put some warm, dry clothes on!

Once Jodi was ready we drove to the indoor arena to ride and work dogs. When we got there we unloaded the horses and cattle but left the dogs in their crates except for the one I wanted to work. I had my truck parked in such a way that I could keep and eye on it. Generally I ask curious people to leave the dogs alone that are still in their crates on the truck, if possible. On this particular day I just happened to be at my truck getting one of the dogs out when this lady walked over. She asked if I had a dog in the crate closest to her. I told her I did but asked her to leave him alone. I explained to her that my dogs had a tendency to get a little wound up listening to the other dogs working cattle and they might bark at her. Unfortunately the lady ignored me and stuck her face about two inches in front of the dog crate door. That poor lady! Hidden Canyon Cross, my young and rambunctious dog, happened to be in the crate. He took a leap at his crate door and barked so loud I bet that lady went straight home and changed her pants. I about died laughing - after she left of course. And that was the end of my laughing for the night.

I walked into the arena to work my dog Sport when the "incident" happened. To this day I still think DQ did it on purpose just to get me in trouble with my wife. I'm not sure exactly how it happened but my wife blamed it all on me. From my perspective it went down like this: Jodi was standing in the arena. When I walked in I told her to go ahead and leave the arena since I was going to work Sport. My guess is that somehow Sport thought I had told him to go get the 6 calves from the other end of the arena and bring them to me. Jodi hadn't gotten out of the arena when DQ saw Sport coming at him. He must have spotted Jodi at the other end of the arena so went running full board toward her. Jodi didn't see him because her back was too him and neither did I because I was watching Sport. The next thing I know that big 650 pound calf had run my little 130 pound wife right over! Jodi was flat on the ground on her back and DQ was standing quietly just a little past her. Oh man alive I knew I was in trouble!

My first concern of course was Jodi. I ran over and asked her if she was okay. That was when I knew I was not going to be okay because of the rather icy tone Jodi used to tell me she was 'FINE'. Sport was standing nearby with this look on his face like 'Did I do good?' All I wanted to do was hide because I knew what was coming next. I refuse to say the words in this book that I heard coming from Jodi. My wife was mad and it stayed that way for the rest of the night! And believe me, I still hear about this! Looking back I just wish we would have named that steer something besides DQ because every time I pass a Dairy Queen I think of that steer and Jodi laying flat on the ground and I cringe just a little bit.

Chapter 8
A Calf on the Wrong Side of the Fence
Summer 2000

I taught my Border Collie Jake to get my calves and bring them to my roping arena when I used to team rope a lot. When I sold Jake I taught my new
dog, Sport, to do the same thing. I would saddle up my horses and tell
Sport to go get my calves. By the time I got to the roping arena Sport
would have them outside the far end of the arena waiting at the gate for me.
I'd ride into the one end of the arena, shut the gate and ride to the other
end where they were waiting. I would open that gate and Sport would herd
them into the stripping chute area, which is where they go when I need to
put on or take off the protective gear wrapping their horns or just need a
secure area to hold them.

One day when I got to the arena the calves weren't there! I thought
heck, this is unusual, Sport always has them waiting for me. I looked around
but I didn't see Sport or my calves anywhere.

I figured I'd better start looking for Sport and the calves so I rode off
into the nearby woods on my horse Badger. A little ways into the woods I
saw Sport just standing there and the calves scattered around. I gave him
the familiar command, "Bring 'em", but he just stood there. What the heck
was going on? Sport was looking at me, trying to tell me something was
wrong. I hollered a couple more times to "Bring 'em" and he still wouldn't
do it. I rode Badger farther into the woods towards Sport and saw this little
blue merle calf that had somehow jumped the fence. He was just standing
there on the wrong side looking at me like he really got away with something! I had no idea what I was going to do. I didn't have a gate back there
because the other side wasn't on my property.

I figured since that little calf jumped the fence, Sport could help him
figure out real quick where he did it and get him back over! I told Sport,
"Go on out" and "Go get him"." Sport shot under the barbed wire fence
and started fighting with that calf trying to get him back on the right side of
the fence. After a minute or two that poor calf decided he didn't want Sport
biting and messing with him anymore so in five seconds flat he was back

where he was supposed to be! I thought how cool it was that Sport could do that. He just knew what I needed him to do!

I told Sport to bring the calves along to the roping arena now that they were all on the right side of the fence. About the time we got to the arena, my roping buddy showed up and I told him I had a little fence fixing to do before we could start roping. He asked me what happened and I told him the whole story. My buddy really wanted to see where this happened so we both rode back into the woods with me carrying my bailing twine so I could tie the barbed wire back together. My buddy said, "That's amazing your dog would just go bring that calf back over the fence like that."

"That dog will do just about anything," I told him. "I got him back there biting on that calf and he figured out how to get him back on the other side of this fence in no time!"

We fixed up the fence and headed back to the arena to enjoy some roping…now that Sport had all the calves where they were supposed to be!

Chapter 9
My Son On The Shale
Summer 2000

I have a friend Scott who lives in Montana and one summer he needed some help rounding up a herd of yearling calves that were way up in the mountains off his ranch. I always like to help Scott out when I can because it's a great time doing what I love – being on horseback and gathering cattle. I decided to take my son Jason with me this time. He was just ten years old and this was his first trip to Montana.

We made the trip from Oregon to Scott's ranch in Montana without any problems. The following day we saddled up the horses and loaded them and Scott's dogs into the trailer and headed off of Scott's property to where the calves were. I didn't bring any of my dogs with me this trip.

We drove up into the mountains, unloaded and started riding around looking for the calves. We figure they were nearby because we were near two watering holes and it was getting hot. "They're going to stay near a water source in this weather." Scott told us. "We'll ride to the watering holes and start looking for tracks." An hour or so later we found some big old steers and tried moving toward them but as soon as they got a hint of us they took off like deer.

We started chasing them and pretty soon we were riding down this hill that was nothing but slippery shale rock. Scott and I were carefully zigzagging down this mountain when I heard the worst commotion I've ever heard. I looked over and saw Jason pulling a "Man from Snowy River" stunt! His horse was flying straight down the mountain, its nose an inch from the ground with Jason tipped so far forward he looked like he was about to bail head over heels! Rocks and shale were flying everywhere! He was scaring the heck out of me! I started screaming at him, "Quick, turn your horse sideways; turn, turn, you're gonna break your neck!"

Of course Jason couldn't hear me. The clatter of the shale was too noisy. The hill was so steep but Jason was just having the time of his life flying down it! I bet he was thinking it had to be the best time he'd had since the carnival was last in town! He finally heard me screaming at him and managed to turn the horse so it was going crosswise down the mountain. He got to the bottom and rode over to us with a big grin on his face!

"You can't do that!" I told him, after the fact of course.

"Man, that was so fun" he said, completely oblivious to his near-death experience.

"Yeah, but you're going to be dead doing stunts like that!" I said in exasperation. He just grinned at me!

Once we'd calmed down after that little stunt, we continued riding across the mountain. After a while we found the calves we were looking for and headed them down the mountain in the right direction. Three or four of them had run through a fence while the others were still on our side. We had to get the ones on the far side of the fence over to our side so we could get them all to the bottom of the hill. We knew if we could get them down there the dogs we brought along would get them stopped.

Scott said, "We can't get the horses over there because of the wire! Darn, we really need those calves on this side of the fence or we're gonna lose them!"

"You know what?" I said, "The calves on this side jumped that fence to be over here so I'll bet those other three will if we can get over to them." Scott stayed back with the dogs and horses while Jason and I went in on foot through the barbed wire fence to get on the back side of those calves. We flicked our hats at them a few times and they jumped right over that fence and took off with the rest of the herd.

I hadn't worked cattle in big country like this before. Once that herd hit the bottom of the mountain and ended up in the big field, Scott put his dogs on them. The dogs got those calves bayed up and under control in no time. It was amazing to watch Scott work his dogs. Using the dogs, we pushed the calves three or four miles down gravel roads to get them back to Scott's part of the ranch. When we got back to the ranch we put them in corrals and loaded them into trailers. Then we loaded up the horses and dogs and took everything back to the main ranch. Scott had semi-trucks coming in to pick up cattle and the calves we just brought in finished up those loads. It was a good day on the ranch!

The skills of horsemanship and dog handling I saw that day were something to watch! At that time I was new to cattle gathering and had never seen anything like what I saw that day. Now I do it!

We do dangerous things "cowboying" that end up being a lot of fun. Most people don't even dream of doing that kind of stuff let alone have the opportunity. They only see it in the movies; movies like "The Man from Snowy River!"

Chapter 10
The Runaway Pony
Summer 2000

My daughter Laura must have been about eleven years old when this incident with the pony happened. I had just gotten myself involved in a little team roping so I was practicing whenever I could. It was one of those really nice summer days, not too hot, and I was out in the driveway with my son Jason roping a roping dummy.

Laura had decided to hook her pony Hershey up to his cart and go for a drive. She had Hershey ready with his harness on but not yet hooked to the cart. She hollered over to me asking for my help in hooking up the cart. So I walked up the hill to help her. We were working on the harness when I noticed there was something missing from the whole getup. I was hooking the cart up to the pony when Laura started to protest about the way I had it. I told her it would work fine the way I had it rigged on the pony. She said no it wouldn't. She said with some authority that someone had told her how she needed to hook it up and it needed to be done a certain way. I explained to her that it would not work the way she was doing it because the cart would hit the pony in the butt and he would run off. So we discussed it for a few more minutes because whoever had told her how to hook it up was a pretty important person to her. The thing is it would have worked the way she was doing it if it weren't for that missing part from the whole getup.

It took some convincing but I finally hooked the cart up to the pony the way I felt it needed to be done and then headed back down the hill to my roping. Little did I know that Laura, convinced I had hooked it up wrong, redid it the way she thought it should be done. Before long she and Hershey were carting all around up at the top of the hill where the shop was. Jason and I couldn't have been roping for more than five minutes when I heard this ear-splitting scream. I looked up just in time to see Hershey and the cart come barreling down the hill at breakneck speed with Laura sitting there screaming at the top of her lungs.

As Hershey and the cart went running by me, maybe about ten feet away, I tried to rope the pony but missed. Thinking back on it, I'm not sure what would have happened if I had caught him because I was on foot and he was running as fast as a pony could go! Once roping him failed I did the next best thing and yelled at Laura to hold on.

Unfortunately Hershey did not go down the driveway but instead went straight off the back side of the shop which was pretty steep and into the lower part of the lawn by the house. This was a two wheeled cart mind you and I swear the tires didn't even touch the ground as they went flying over that steep section. They hit in the bottom of the lawn and Laura was still screaming. I was still yelling at her to hold on.

At the bottom of the lawn there were three options for Hershey; turn, hit the fence or stop. I sure was hoping he would stop but every time he tried the cart would hit him in the butt. Well, Hershey decided to turn. He, the cart and Laura went careening across the bottom lawn. Then the pony turned and started back up the hill. As he was heading back up the hill he had to get on the driveway again and go past me. As they sailed by me for a second time I could see Laura's eyes and they were about as big as baseballs!

There was nothing I could do at this point except watch as the tires went off the ground again when that cart bounced onto the driveway. This time though, Hershey turned down the driveway and headed out to the gravel road we lived on. My wife Jodi was in the garden which was alongside of the driveway and she watched in horror as Hershey, the cart and a screaming Laura went racing by. I screamed at Jodi that I was getting the truck. I knew we couldn't keep up with this pony on foot. He looked like he was going to leave the country to get away from that cart!

I ran to my truck, started it and took off after the runaway pony. When I got to the gravel road I could see the pony running as hard as he could up the road. Luckily for us he was going uphill. He ran about an eighth of a mile and I caught up with them about the time he stopped. I got out of my truck and carefully approached Hershey, saying "Whoa" over and over. All I wanted was to get hold of him before he tried to turn around and head back for home and downhill! I was able to get hold of the driving lines finally, then I had to pry Laura's little hands off the cart. She had lost her glasses but she was okay. Jodi and Jason showed up about that time. We got Hershey and the cart back to the house and we all had a good laugh. As far as that missing piece went, I never did find out what it was but I'm guessing it kept the cart from bumping the pony in the butt. After that experience however, Laura decided she liked riding the pony instead of being in the cart!

Chapter 11
Hangin' Tree Sport
Fall 2000

There came a point early on in my work with cow dogs when I decided I wanted to buy a Hangin' Tree cow dog from Gary Erickson. He's the fellow who developed the breed standard and raises them in his home state of Oklahoma. The main problem I faced was taking the time to get there from Oregon. But, when I made up my mind I had to have one of these dogs, nothing else would do. I first flew to Texas to recruit some family help. I have a nephew, Larry who lives there. I knew Larry had a truck and I was pretty sure he would be willing to take a drive up to Oklahoma with me. As I suspected, it didn't take me long to talk him into going with me and meeting Gary about some dogs.

We left out of Huntsville, Texas the evening after I arrived and drove non-stop to Oklahoma. When we were getting close I called Gary.

"We probably won't get there until eleven or so tonight. My nephew Larry and I are going to get a hotel room and we'll come up to your place in the morning." I told him.

"No, no, no," Gary said. "You just come on in tonight and you can bunk here at the house."

I accepted Gary's hospitality and Larry and I kept on driving. We arrived right about 11 pm, just as I thought we would.

I'll be darned if we didn't walk into Gary's house and his wife had hot, home-cooked food on the table waiting for us! We visited and got to know each other a little better over our delicious late-night meal. Shortly thereafter we went to bed; full, tired, and very grateful for the hospitality.

Early the next morning Gary called for us. Larry and I went outside and watched him work some of his dogs. When he took a break I told him, "Gary, I want a male dog to use for a stud dog and preferably one with a real nice temperament." He walked me over to a pen with probably 20 or so pups in it and asked "Well, what are you thinking."

"I don't know, you tell me." I said as I watched all those little pups play together. "Which dog would you take for a stud dog prospect?" Gary pointed to a little black pup. "Great! I'll take him." And just like that I had myself a Hangin' Tree Cowdog!

The rest of the morning we spent working cows with some older pups and I ended up buying one of those also. She was a year old pup and her name was Smoke. Now I had two new dogs!

Gary's wife called us in to breakfast about that time and it was another fine, home-cooked meal! After breakfast we thanked them both and said good bye. Larry and I loaded the two pups in the truck and took off back to Huntsville, Texas. From Texas I put the dogs in kennels and flew them home to Oregon.

I ended up naming the younger of the pups, Sport. What a dog! In the beginning he could get out of anything. I mean it didn't matter what it was; I would put him in my pens and he would escape in no time. It got to whenever I would hear the other dogs howling and yelping I would know - Sport was out again!

I started working with Sport right away. At first the only thing I trained him to do was bring me cattle. I didn't know a whole lot about training dogs at that time and I didn't realize how important it was to teach him other things! He also continued getting out of his pen and it seemed like it was always two or three in the morning when that happened. The other dogs would start making a racket, barking and howling, and I would go outside and Sport would be gone! I would go traipsing up to the woods in the pitch dark to find him. Most of the time he would have my roping steers bayed up in the corner!

I had taught him NOT to come to me and to always stay on the back side of the cattle. Because I had taught him so well, I couldn't catch him! When he would escape late at night like he usually did, I would be out there with a little kid's rope and a flashlight. I would hold the flashlight in my mouth and try to rope Sport when he'd come around some corner or would race by. I'm sure it was a pretty funny site seeing me out there at two in the morning with a flashlight in my mouth and cussing at the same time! Eventually I would catch him, come back to the house and hopefully get some sleep before I had to go out and catch him again!

This went on for several months. I finally figured out by trial and error that I'd better teach him to come to me any time I called! That is now something I do with all of my dogs to this day and quite early on! I also make sure my kennels are built a little stronger so my dogs don't escape!

I worked and trained Sport for a long time. That dog could do everything but drive my truck! Everywhere I went people wanted me to train their kids like that dog! I usually refused that request but I could tell some kids probably could have used it! For me, I had to learn how to train my dogs the hard way, through trial and error and sometimes very late at night! But, I learned how to train my dogs well!

Chapter 12
How I Started Raising Cattle Master Cow Dogs
2002

Some people say I'm a little bit crazy about driving because I'll take off and drive from Oregon to Texas and not think much about it. One year I had a litter of pups I was going to sell to Scott, a buddy of mine who lived over in Montana. My son Jason, who was about twelve years old, wanted to come along so I decided we'd make it a fun trip by stopping at this big horse sale in Laramie, Wyoming called the *'Come to the Source Horse Sale'*. I was pretty excited to do this because I was looking for a nice blue roan Quarter Horse. Our plan was to first stop off at Scott's house and sell him a couple puppies then head to the horse sale.

When we arrived in Montana Scott bought a couple pups but there were a few left. We happened to be sitting out on the front porch catching up on our cattle stories, at that pretty time of day when it's just starting to get dark, when Scott said, "Man, did you see that article about these cow dogs called Cattle Masters?"

"No, I never heard of them." I replied.

He got the magazine and showed me the article and I read it. The article described the breed as a mix of Border Collie, Kelpie and American Bull Dog.

"I sure wouldn't mind having one of these pups."

"Well you should call that guy." Scott encouraged.

"Well, shoot… Me and Jason are heading to Wyoming in a few days. Texas is the wrong way." I paused and thought about this for a moment.

Scott quickly threw in, "I bet that guy, Charlie, who's down in Kansas, will buy the rest of those pups from you. Kansas can be on your way to Texas."

I called Charlie and let him know I had three nice pups I was trying to sell. He said he would buy them because he knew about my Hangin' Tree Cowdogs.

I asked Jason, "Do you want to go to Texas?"

"Yeah, I've always wanted to go to Texas." I could tell he was excited about the prospect of a road trip.

"Then I think that's what we'll do. We'll go to Texas." As an afterthought I added, "Of course that's depending if this ol' boy has any of those Cattle Master Dogs left to sell!"

"Cool! But what about the horse sale?" Jason asked.

"We'll go next year." I didn't think Jason minded too much since he already had a nice horse of his own back home.

So I called this fellow from Texas who was in the article Scott had showed me. He told me he still had a few Cattle Masters left to sell. Jason and I decided then and there we were going!

The next morning we started out on our trip down south. I'd driven trucks my whole life all over the country but for some reason I couldn't read the maps we bought! I thought I had dirt in my eyes or something. I had to get Jason to read them. We didn't have all those navigators and GPS's back then like we have nowadays.

Jason helped read the maps and we got down the road by and by but boy was it hot! We had these little pups with us and it was the middle of August and hot! I mean it was HOT! We decided it was time to find a hotel room for the rest of the evening and cool off; hopefully one that liked pups! We for sure couldn't leave them in the truck in all that heat.

We finally found a little place that let us bring those pups inside. Poor Jason ended up staying up most of the night. He had to sit down on the floor so he could keep the pups from crying while I could get some sleep!

The next morning we got up early and took off. We drove the rest of the way to Charlie's house in Kansas. Like he promised, he bought those last three pups I had and soon after we were headed for Texas.

Once in Texas, we meet up with this guy from the article named Jason. As it turned out, he only had one dog at his place named Uno. I was curious and asked him how the dog got its name.

"Well, the mom only had one pup," he said, "and that's Uno!"

"Well," I said, "I'll buy him."

From there Jason sent us over to this other guy's house and I bought a pup from him too. Now we had two Cattle Master pups. I figured it was time to head back to Oregon so my son and I made our way home.

Every year since 2002, I've planned to go to that *'Come to the Source Horse Show'*. Yet somehow I never manage to make it! Every year I get turned the wrong way or something else happens and it gets put off for another year! Come to think of it though, missing that horse sale is how I got started raising Cattle Master Dogs!

Chapter 13
The Long-Horned Bull
2002

One day I got a frantic phone call from a guy named Earl.

"Marvin, I've got a bull running loose around Dayton that I need you to catch for me" he blurts out first thing.

Anytime I get a phone call about catching a bull, right away I'm thinking it's going to be ornery, it's going to be a fight and I'm going to have fun!

"Well, give me the scoop. What's going on with him?" I asked.

"It's a long–horned bull and weighs 'bout eight or nine hundred pounds. He's special and all, registered you know, and he's our prize show bull!"

It just so happens that my son Jason is also my best help. He can ride a horse, handle a rope, work with the dogs or do whatever I need him to do. Plus, being that he's thirteen and it's summer time, he's usually always around. I knew right off the bat that I was going to need help on this job so I went home to find Jason.

"Hey," I hollered out to him when I caught sight of him up by the barn. "There's a bull out in Dayton we need to catch." That got his attention. "This guy called me and wants us to come and catch him. It seems nobody's been able to so far. Guy says he's in the brush somewhere down by a creek." I paused to let him get a good picture of this in his head, "Do you want to help?"

Not a bit of hesitation. "Sure."

Of course Jason is always ready to help me. He never knows what trouble we're going to get into but he always knows it's going to be exciting whatever it is!

Jason got his horse, Comet, ready. I saddled up my horse Badger and got Sport, my Hangin' Tree Cowdog, from the kennel. We loaded everyone in the truck and trailer and took off for Dayton.

We met up with Earl at his place. I asked him where the bull was. It always helps if you have some idea of where they are to start!

"Well, I don't know," Earl said. "I think he's down there in that creek bottom somewhere."

"You haven't seen him?" I asked, a little surprised. This was going to be interesting!

"No, not for awhile. At least a couple days I think...."

I was thinking *'oh boy, this is definitely going to be interesting if not a bit challenging*!

Jason and I unloaded the horses and Sport, cinched up our saddles, then took off riding toward the creek after Earl pointed us in the right direction.

We rode around for some time but couldn't find this bull anywhere. We eventually came to the creek and saw an old rickety bridge that went across. I was not about to put my horse on it to get to the other side. Especially considering the creek below the bridge was twenty feet down and the bank was super steep.

I suggested to Jason, "Hey, how about we go back up the hill, load up and drive around the backside of this property to the next road over and see if we can find him on the other side of this bridge?" Jason thought that might be a good idea.

We rode back up the hill and loaded the horses and dog in the trailer. Earl was up there waiting for us. I asked him, "How can we get to the other side of that creek?" He pointed to my left and started to tell me how to drive the two or three miles around to the other side then decided he'd just come along with us so he climbed up into the truck.

We drove to the other side of the creek where there were fields all around and a big nursery. "Just park anywhere." Earl said. "You can ride around down to that creek bottom from here. I'll wait up here by the truck." We ended up parking the trailer near the nursery, got the dog and horses ready and rode down to the creek bottom.

As we started towards the bottom we realized there was no way we could get through all the brush and thickets with the horses to the creek bottom so Jason volunteered, "I'll walk down in there."

"Ok, but you be careful. This is supposed to be a pretty mean bull with big horns!" I continued, "If you see that bull holler and if he gets after you sic Sport on him."

Jason and Sport went down through the brush to the creek bottom and soon enough I heard Jason hollering and screaming. He found that bull all right.

"He's in the corner down here in the brush and he can't get out unless he runs over me." Jason yelled up to me.

"Don't let him run over you. Get on out of there and we'll figure it out." I hollered back, a bit nervous because I didn't want Jason run over.

Thankfully Jason quickly climbed out of the brush with Sport and came hustling back toward me. Jason was pretty darn excited he found the bull so I asked him, "What do you think?" Even though Jason was only thirteen, I trusted his opinion because we'd done this so many times together that he'd acquired a good gut feeling about how to handle tough situations. "Do you think we can go down there and rope him? Can we get him out of there?" I asked.

"I don't think we can get him out this way. He just has to go across that old bridge." Jason told me.

"Well let's go look at it and take some ropes." I suggested.

We left the horses tied to some trees and walked on down toward the creek with Sport. We saw the bull holed up down there and sure enough, he was bayed up in a corner back in the brush.

"I think I'll sic Sport on him and bring him out of there. The only place he can go is across that bridge." I said, outlining my plan to Jason.

We set ourselves up and then I set Sport on that bull. Sport ran at him, biting, barking and fighting and sure enough he ran out of the brush but he stopped short at the bridge. He came right up to it but he just balked then bayed up by the side of it in some more brush. I turned to Jason and said, "I think we'll need to rope him. Let's tie a couple of ropes together, run them across that bridge, and tie the bull to the tree that's over there. That should hold him while we get the horses and the truck and get around to the other side. Then once over there we'll work out the rest of the plan!"

Jason was almost falling down laughing. He thought this was pretty funny. Trying to get sixty feet of rope on this bull was like having a skier on the end of a rope tied to a truck with a maniac driving! But that was the plan and that was what we did! Jason and I got to running that bull back and forth with my dog and it was pretty comical. One of us finally threw a rope on him! Then we tied two ropes together and Jason ran across the bridge to the other side and tied the rope to a tree. Now at least we had the bull caught!

The next part of the plan involved walking back up the hill, untying our horses, riding them to the truck and loading them up again. Once at the truck we told Earl what was going on. I think he was wondering what the heck we thought we were going to do! We drove back around to Earl's property on the other side of the creek and parked the truck. Of course we couldn't get the truck anywhere near the bridge because of the brush so no chance of loading him right from there. And, to top it off, the corral where Earl wanted us to put him was one-half to three-quarters of a mile from where we were.

Earl stepped out of the truck and asked, "Now where'd you say that bull was?"

"He's tied to a tree down there but the tree is on this side of the bridge and he's on the other side." Earl started laughing.

"Well what are you going to do now?" he asked me.

"Well, we're gonna go down there with our horses and dog and I'm going to dally him off to my saddle horn. Then I'll sic my dog on him and the only choice he'll have is to cross that bridge!" Jason and I set up down there on the one side of the bridge with our horses. I dallied the bull off on my saddle horn once I get the rope untied from the tree. That bull was standing on the other side of that bridge just staring at us. I sent Sport across the bridge to start biting on him. It probably took ten minutes of biting, cussing, laughing, hollering, pulling and barking before Sport convinced that bull to cross the bridge. I guided him along with the rope and my horse!

Once the bull was on the side I needed him to be, I untied the two ropes so I only had the one length of rope to deal with. I dallied the end of this shorter rope to my saddle and walked the bull toward the corral Earl wanted him in. Jason followed up behind us using Sport to keep the bull moving. Unfortunately it was a fight the whole way. The bull didn't want to go and he let us know in no uncertain terms! We finally got to the corral and my horse was just walking through the gate when my rope broke right at the steel Hondo on the end.

The minute that rope broke and slid off the bull's neck, he turned and took off, right through a neighbor's garden! Luckily Jason had a loop ready. He rode right up behind the bull and they were both just tearing through this garden. Dirt clods were flying everywhere! Jason swung his rope but missed. I tied a big Hondo on to the end of my rope and took off after the bull. By this time he was running through someone else's yard, across the road, and out into this big grass field. Jason's horse, Comet, who is really fast, caught up with the bull and Jason got him roped and stopped right as I came loping up on Badger. The rope was tied around Jason's saddle horn and the bull was bawling and fighting and really putting some strain on Jason's saddle.

"You want to bring him back?" I asked.

"No," Jason exclaims. "You take him. I don't want to fight him." Couldn't say I blamed him!

It took us another five or ten minutes to get the bull back to the corral and as we neared the gate he ran in like he was overjoyed to find his long lost home! I guess he had enough of me, my horses, my dog, my son, everything! He just wanted in his corral and in his barn. We managed to quickly get the rope off him and happily shut the gate.

Earl was standing there at the corral watching this whole situation unfold. I could see he was just so tickled we caught his bull.

"Man, I'm sorry about your garden," I told him.

"Awe, that's all right. It's not even my garden - it's the neighbors. They just got it planted but no worries. They can re-sow whatever they need!"

I was wondering if the neighbors were going to take it so casually that their garden had been completely destroyed! Well, I figured they were Earl's neighbors; he's the one who's got to live with them next door.

Jason and I rode out of there and back to our truck and trailer.

"Jason, this is fun stuff. What more can a guy ask for. The only thing that would make it better is if Jodi and Laura were here." I was thinking my wife and daughter would have had fun on this one. "We're out riding, just the two of us, instead of doing something that's dull and boring or getting in trouble. We're getting paid for doing what we love to do; riding our horses, roping cattle and working our dog." Jason couldn't agree more with me! As I put Sport into his dog box on the back of my truck I gave him a scratch behind the ears. He sure was a special dog. I didn't know if we could have done this without him!

Chapter 14
How We Got Our Dog "Cross"
Summer 2002

Back when I first took an interest in cow dogs, I bought two Hangin' Tree Cowdogs, Smoke and Sport, from a well-known breeder named Gary in Oklahoma. A few years later my wife, Jodi, and I went back to Oklahoma and met up with Choc, Gary's son, who had been helping him with his Hangin' Tree Cowdog business. I wanted to talk to Choc about buying another dog and pup.

One day while we were watching Choc work some dogs. I said, "Well Choc, I sure wouldn't mind having another dog."

"You know what Marvin," Choc started to say as he stopped for a break "I have a dog in Colorado named Bob who's about a year and a half old. I sold him to this guy out there and man, he's one tough dog. The guy got him started working on cow-calf pairs but he's got to barking so much that he isn't bringing the cows in. He's just balling them up and holding them." Choc paused for a moment, thinking. Jodi and I waited, wondering where this was going. "You know, I sent that guy his money back but I need to find a way to get that dog picked up. If you want to swing back through Colorado on your way home to Oregon, you and your wife can have him."

I quickly responded, "Heck yeah, that's worth a try and its beautiful country out that way…worth the drive."

We stayed in Oklahoma a couple more days and worked dogs with Choc. I ended up buying a dog and two pups from Choc before Jodi and I headed to Colorado to pick up Bob. We went through Denver, then Vale, before calling the guy who had Bob and making arrangements to meet up with him.

When we met we talked about Bob. This guy told me all about the problems he was having with the dog. Basically he just couldn't get along with Bob. He told me "I like my dogs to go up on the sides of the mountain and bring the cattle to me while I ride down in the canyons. That way I can keep pushing them with my horse. I did this with Bob for a few weeks but he got to fighting the cattle too much and circling them up on the mountain instead of bringing them down."

I thanked this guy for the information about Bob, told him I'd keep it in mind as I worked with him then shook his hand. Jodi and I loaded up Bob and headed back to Oregon.

Once we were home and I started working with Bob I could see what that guy had meant. Bob did bark all the time but he was also tough; a real "head" kind of dog which meant he liked getting right up in a cows face to take a hold of its head. I could tell he wanted to listen and he wanted to work. Since I had that dog Smoke I'd gotten from Gary, and since Smoke was a female, I had an idea and I mentioned it to Jodi one day, "I think I'll breed those two dogs." I just thought they would make some great pups.

We ended up getting a good litter from those two dogs, Smoke and Bob. Jodi wanted to keep one so we held on to a little pup that was black with a white cross on its neck. We naturally just started calling him Cross and soon that became his name. His full registered name was Hidden Canyon Cross. We also liked to call him Mutt-Face because he had a big ol' head on him!

Cross was a great dog but he was real strong headed, kind of like his daddy. He just wanted to eat cows alive! Jodi had him for probably a year but he got to be too much dog for her. Eventually I came up with an idea I thought she might like.

I said, "Jodi, I bought this dog, Tren, from a lady and I think she might be a great dog for you. So, I'll tell you what, I'll trade you dogs."

"All right, you've got a deal!" She responded, somewhat relieved to be getting rid of Cross.

She still has Tren and this was ten years ago. That dog sleeps by her bed every night and works cows in the day. She loves to play and she's been the best dog ever for Jodi.

What was really neat about Cross is that Jodi and I raised him well and he turned into an amazing cow dog. Because of his abilities as a cow dog he was in demand as a sire. Now there are dogs all over the United States who carry his bloodlines!

Chapter 15
Hangin' Tree Sport and
The Steer Roping Lesson
Summer 2002

My dog, Hangin' Tree Sport was the best dog a person could ever have. I will probably say that over and over throughout my stories. I had him for eleven years and besides being an outstanding cow dog, he was also my buddy.

Before I bought Sport I had a Border Collie, Jake, but I sold him. I was still fairly new at training cow dogs but I wanted to teach Sport to be just as good of a cow dog as Jake had been.

My son Jason and I were out in our arena team roping one day. Jason couldn't have been more than eleven at the time. Sport was with us and I was planning on teaching Sport to lie down and stay while we roped. I had him lay down by a gate up at the head box. I happened to be riding a young colt named Buddy that I had recently started under saddle. I should have known better than to ride that colt around a pup that I was trying to train!

Jason was heeling and I was doing the heading that day. Jason opened the chute and the roping steer took off down the arena. I ran after it on my young colt. I roped the steer and turned left, which is what you are supposed to do in team roping. My son was coming in with his rope to heel him. As I was turning left I could see that Jason was staying too far back. I started hollering at him, "Jason, kick it up!" Basically I was telling him to get closer to the steer and rope him. "I can't," he yelled back, "Sport's in there." Sport had decided to be my heeler for some reason. He ran up and bit this steer on the back leg. I guess Sport was thinking I wanted the steer to keep up with me. My rope, around the steer's head at this point, was off to the right side of my horse where it belonged but as the steer got bit by Sport he swung back behind and over to the left side of my horse. When he did this the rope had nowhere to go but under my horses tail!

I'm not even sure how to paint this picture but my horse started bucking really hard. I was being bounced up out of the saddle and went so high that I ended up standing on the saddle! Right away I leapt down on the ground with my rope and my horse's reins still in my hand! Luckily the steer was one of the smaller ones so when he came running by in front of me I grabbed him by the rope and got him stopped.

Jason was across the arena laughing so hard he almost fell off his horse. Sport was lying on the ground waiting for the next moment to help me some more. I just give him this look that said I don't need his help anymore, that's for sure!

I finally got the rope unwound off the saddle horn and got the steer to stand still long enough for my horse to get his tail eased up so the rope could fall loose. I let the steer go and Jason and I had a good laugh over the whole thing.

After that I learned to put my dog on a barrel. If you get a dog to lie on a barrel instead of on the ground it's easier for them to learn to stay. That way, if the dog moves they know they have done something wrong because it's easy for them to tell they're not in the same spot. If they're just on the ground they tend to start crawling and inching forward and before you know it they're off at a run. In hindsight, I think I was actually the one who had the lesson that day!

Chapter 16
Letting My Under-Age Son Drive My Truck
June 2003

I was asked to do a cow dog demonstration at a fund-raiser Poker Ride in Molalla, Oregon one summer. I didn't have enough room for my horses and cattle in the same load so I left the horses at home for the second trip. When my son Jason and I arrived with my calves I put them in a corral I was told I could use before the demo started. Since I'd already checked to make sure everything was set up and all the gates were shut, I unloaded the calves. As it happened, I had this Jersey calf with me that I suspected was mentally handicapped. I don't mean that in any disrespectful way. I think he just had some mental problems. He would follow you everywhere if you happened to be walking around him. If you weren't careful he would follow your horse. I don't think he even knew he was a cow!

As the calves unloaded they had to travel down this paneled-off lane to get to their corral. Well somebody at the Poker Ride had opened the gate at the far end of the lane sometime after I had checked them all. I had five calves, four of which went into the corral that branched off the lane but this Jersey calf went right on by and out the open gate at the end of the lane. I guess he was planning on going on the poker ride with everybody!

Of course I didn't have any dogs with me. I didn't even have my horse! I had planned to head back home after dropping off the calves so we could pick up our horses, the dogs and anything else I thought we might need. That's why I didn't even have my rope!

Well, this Jersey calf took off down a trail. I was running around trying to find somebody with a rope that would help me rope him and tie him to a tree. I was following along behind this calf on foot but there was no way I could get him stopped. He just kept trucking along and all the while people's horses were bucking and running off because some of them weren't used to cattle. And they were sure not used to a calf coming at them! This calf wasn't exactly little; he probably weighed six or seven hundred pounds.

That poor calf was just looking for a friend and nobody wanted to be his friend.

Finally I found this guy who had a rope. "Man, would you rope this calf for me and tie it to that tree?" I asked him.

"You bet!" he said. Boy was I relieved!

We ended up getting this calf roped and tied to a tree. I told Jason, "Let's run back and get my truck and trailer and we'll drive down here to throw him in the trailer." We pulled up with the trailer and it took us about two minutes to get him in. Then we drove back to the corral and unloaded him with the rest of the calves. Finally Jason and I headed back to our house in Newberg to get the rest of our stuff. We loaded the horses and dogs in record time then headed back to Molalla just in time to start our cow dog demonstration.

I had Sport with me to work the cows in the demonstration so, as usual, everything was going great. Jason was twelve years old at that time and I really didn't think much about him driving the truck and trailer a little here and there. He'd actually been driving my truck a bit since he was nine. I didn't know how many hundreds of people were at this event but I didn't really think about it when I said, "Hey Jason, will you run out to the parking lot and get my truck and trailer and bring it in so we can load the cattle?"

Jason ran out to get the truck and trailer. He had to sit on the edge of the seat because he couldn't see over the steering wheel. Soon enough he pulled into the arena driving my truck with the trailer behind it.

I worked the calves with the dogs for a few minutes then I demonstrated to the audience how easy it was to load them in the trailer with the dogs. Once they were loaded, I threw my horse in the back section, and I drove out of the arena to park the truck and trailer.

Jason and I were talking as we walked back up into the stands. They were giving out the prizes for the poker hands from the ride. As we sat down a lady came over to me with a very serious look on her face. I was thinking I must be in trouble for something. Maybe she was bucked off her horse when my calf got loose or something. She said, "Sir, I need to ask you, do you think it's a good idea to let your boy drive that big truck and trailer in the arena?"

I had to pause and think about that for a moment before I said to her, "You know really, I never even gave it a thought. He drives all the time. He probably drives better than a lot of the people that are in this parking lot right now!"

"Well I just don't think it's a good idea." she angrily stated.

"You know, you have your right to think that and I understand where you're coming from. I wouldn't let most kids I know drive my truck and trailer. The only reason he doesn't drive my truck and trailer down the highway when we're on a road trip is because he's so little he can't see over the steering wheel without sitting on the edge of the seat." I watched as her face started turning red and she began to protest. Hoping to appease her, I quickly added, "Oh…and he doesn't have a driver's license!"

Chapter 17
Herding the Hogs
Summer 2003

This is the kind of story you only tell years after it happened. One hot day I was outside busy with some chore when my wife Jodi found me and then informed me that our three hogs were gone.

"What do you mean gone?" I asked.

So she explained it to me again in two words, "They're gone!"

"Well where did they go?"

Jodi very firmly said, "If I knew that I wouldn't be coming to you for help! So in other words, I have no idea!"

So, the hunt to find these hogs began. It only took about ten minutes or so before we found them about 400 yards away. They were actually still on our property but only because they hadn't made it to the back fence yet. Unfortunately the back fence was only three loose strands of barbed wire. The grass where they were rooting around was about two feet tall and boy were those hogs happy! But I wasn't happy! I had things to do and it had nothing to do with rounding up hogs in the heat! Jodi said they'd follow her so she grabbed some grass and called to them. They followed her to the first gate but decided they sure weren't going any further.

Well if you know me you know I train cattle dogs so what did I do? I walked back to the kennels and pulled out my two best cow dogs, Hangin' Tree Sport and Hidden Canyon Cross.

Working hogs out in the middle of a field is not easy work as I soon discovered. I'm not sure if you can really dog-break hogs but I could tell you those three hogs were not dog broke! So, the fight began. I got behind the hogs and tried to head them back to the barn lot and their pen. I had used both dogs to catch and hold calves many, many times but neither of them had ever tried working hogs. This only meant I had nothing going in my favor!

My wife really liked these hogs so the first words out of her mouth were, "Don't let the dogs hurt those hogs!" After about 30 minutes of fighting with the hogs I was so hot, sweaty, and mad I didn't much care about those hogs. I just wanted them in their pen so I could get back to what I was doing. Needless to say, my dogs were hot and tired too and probably hoping to make short work of this.

Since the hogs wouldn't leave the field I decided I'd have the dogs bite them just a little. My first mistake was saying "Bite 'em" to both the dogs when the hogs turned the wrong way. Sport bit the first one and let go but not Cross. He usually bit hard and didn't like to let go! The hog that Cross latched on to was not happy! My wife started hollering at me but I was so mad by then I didn't care about her hogs. Quickly I yelled at Cross "That'll do" and he let go of the hog. Now the hogs were headed in the right direction so all was well. I was thinking to myself how I should have had the dogs do a little biting right from the start!

When the hogs walked up to the barn lot gate, two of them walked right through but one turned back. All I had to say was "Bite 'em" and that hog had my two dogs on his head. Now my wife was really screaming at me and the hog was squealing like crazy. I won't say here the words that came out of my mouth other then I didn't care about that darn hog right then. All I wanted was for him to get in the pen! That hog turned to the gate so I told my dogs "That'll do" and they let go of him.

Two of those hogs, the smart ones, had enough of the dogs. They just wanted in their pen and to be left alone. But that one stubborn hog, all he wanted was to make my life miserable! And he was doing a good job of it too!

When we got up to the pen the two smart hogs ran in but the one trying to make me miserable turned to make one last attempt at escaping. In a flash he had two dogs on him. Again the hog was squealing, my wife was screaming and I was telling my dogs, "Bite him" some more! It ended quickly as that hog turned back to the pen and ran in to join his buddies.

After all was said and done, the hogs were back in their pen and everyone was fine. My wife and I finally had a good laugh over the whole ordeal.

Chapter 18
The Cow Who Wore Bailing Twine
Winter 2004

I had this cow once who was about the meanest bovine a person could have. She always wanted to kill my dogs. She was "fighting-mean" protective of her calves too, even after they were weaned.

One day I decided to call my neighbor, Fred, about her. We owned several cows together that we kept over on his property. I asked him, "Hey Fred, would you mind if I put this cow in with the rest of our herd over at your place to raise her calf?" He was agreeable to this.

Shortly after I spoke with him I took her over to his property and turned her out. A few days later he called me and said, "Marvin, this cow has bailing twine twisted all around her horns and I can't get close enough to her to get it off." Bailing twine is used to wrap hay bales but more often than not it ends up loose and lying around all over the barn and out in the fields.

"I'll come over and rope her down then cut off that bailing twine." I told Fred.

I asked my son, Jason, if he wanted to help me with this mean cow. "Sure," he said. It was the middle of winter and the weather that day was really bad; rainy, cold, foggy and slopping wet mud. I don't know why, but we decided to do this anyway on that particular day. My brother Jim happened to be in town from Texas and I got this bright idea, "Hey Jim, how would you like to tape this thing for me? It'll be fun to watch!"

"Well, okay." he said.

Jason and I loaded our horses into the trailer, grabbed Sport from his kennel, then drove over to Fred's property to remove the twine off the cow. We parked on the top of the hill in this big field and rode out to get her. Jim sat inside the truck with his camcorder set on the window ready to video the whole thing.

Jason and I ended up running around in this field like a bunch of wild Indians trying to rope this one cow. It was wet and mud was flying everywhere! The whole herd of cows wouldn't bay up worth a darn because I hadn't been over to Fred's working them with my dogs as much as I needed to. I finally got a rope around this cow's head and got her dallied off to my saddle horn. I wanted to get her close to the truck so Jim could video it. It was so foggy I could barely see where the truck was.

Jason and I, with the help of Sport, finally drug the cow near the truck where Jason could get her back feet roped. We stretched her out and got her down on the ground. I got off of my horse and grabbed a hold of her head. It was a bit of a fight with her because she thrashed about but I managed to cut all the bailing twine off her head. We turned her loose and went back to the truck. "Jim, did you get all that on video?"

"Yeah, I did," he said. "You guys looked pretty funny out there slopping in the mud like that just to cut some twine off that mean old cow's head!"

Later I watched the video Jim made. The visual effect was amazing because of the way we kept rolling out of the fog and into focus on the screen. One of these days I'm going to put it on my website so everyone can enjoy watching it.

Chapter 19
Fish For Dinner
June 2004

During the summers, my wife, kids and I would drive to Montana where we would help my buddy Scott with the cattle on his ranch. Normally we would work three or four days on cattle then we'd ride up to the high lakes to trout fish, camp and relax.

On one of these summer vacations we had finished up with the cattle work and were ready to enjoy the camping and relaxing part of the vacation. We got up early in the morning and loaded everything we'd need in the trucks and trailers. This included the dogs, horses, gear, kids, and grub. Between me and Scott we had ten dogs we were taking with us. We wanted the dogs to have fun and some time off too from all the hard cattle work!

We drove the trucks up as far as we could then unloaded the horses. That year Scott's son, Clay, happened to be going with us. Clay was only about five years old so Scott had to get his bay horse saddled up for him. He plopped Clay up in the saddle on that bay horse, handed me the reins and said, "Hold on to Clay's horse. I got to get my horse saddled and then ready."

Scott went back to the trailer to fetch the horse he was going to ride. He led this horse a little ways away from us and saddled him up. Then without any further fussing, he swung up in the saddle. The moment he set himself down in that saddle his horse started bucking like crazy! Scott just stuck to him like a burr and bucked him out about 75 yards! It was a regular rodeo! I knew we were all thinking "Holy Cow!" Or at least I was! The horse finished bucking and Scott rode over to us saying, "Ok, he's good for the rest of the day! Let's go!"

"Man, do you go through this every time?" I asked, a bit surprised by what just went on.

"Every morning," he said.

"I'd trade that horse in for a bicycle or something if it was me!"

Scott just laughed. I think he might have actually liked that horse!

We had a nice ride up to the high lakes; it's just beautiful country out that way. It was June and there was just enough snow melt that we were able to get the horses up to the lakes. We rode for about two hours. There was dead fall from trees everywhere blocking our trail but we were able to ride around it. At one point along the trail we came across a pretty good sized tree blocking our path. We tried and tried but couldn't find a way to ride around it. Fortunately we happened to have ropes with us because we always carry them, but no one had thought to bring a saw!

Scott said, "Well, looks like we're just not going to get there this year."

"Oh, we're going to get there," I adamantly said. "We rode this far and we're gonna go fishing. Let's put our ropes around that log and see if we can break that tree up."

"We can't break that tree Marvin!"

"Well, I'm not leaving without trying!" We put two or three ropes around the tree and dallied them to our saddle horns. Then we started pulling…and kept pulling. We heard a big 'SNAP' and knew our effort paid off! We were now able to break the rest of the tree apart and finish our ride to the lake.

After we unpacked our gear, got the animals settled and set up camp we settled in to do some serious fishing and it was a blast. Every cast caught a fish! We fished for an hour or so before deciding it was time to do a little cooking. Nothing tastes better than fresh caught trout cooked over an open fire.

Scott, Jason and I walked over to a little stream that fed into the lake where we could clean our fish. We all lined up along the stream so we could work with some efficiency. We would grab a fish, get it cleaned, lay it out behind us then grab the next one off the line to clean. We cleaned about eight or ten fish before I just happened to look behind me. And there the dogs were, standing in a line behind us eating the fish as fast as we cleaned them! As soon as we laid a fish down they were eating it! We ran those dogs off so we could at least eat the few fish we had left! I guess they thought if they were camping with us they got to eat what we did too! Sure beat dog food.

Chapter 20
One Little Donkey
Summer 2004

I was building fence one summer for these people who had several little donkeys on their property. For the longest time I'd wanted to get a donkey for me and the kids to practice roping with. So one day when I was out there I asked the lady if she wanted to sell one but she wasn't interested in doing that. However, she did say I could use one of them. I told her that would be great and I would pick it up the next day. I couldn't wait to have a donkey for us to practice our roping.

The next morning I was excited to get the donkey so I quickly hooked up the trailer. Just as I was getting ready to head out I decided to take Jake, my Border Collie, along with me. He loved to go wherever I went.

As I was heading out the door I mentioned to my wife I was going to bring back a little donkey I had borrowed. Of course she thought I was crazy but that wasn't going to stop me.

When I arrived at the property there was no one around to help me catch the donkey but I knew where they were so I drove to the field and backed up to the gate.

When I got out of the truck I let Jake out too. I knew he would stay out of the way and out of trouble. I walked into the field to get my donkey but he ran off the moment he saw me coming toward him and I thought this was not good because it was already getting hot! I tried to corner him but that didn't work. I kept trying to catch him but was having no luck. Meanwhile, Jake was laying under a tree in the shade happily watching me chase this little donkey around.

After another thirty minutes in the hot sun I walked over to the truck and got a rope. Then it really got crazy as I tried to rope a little miniature donkey in a field on foot! This wasted another thirty minutes and by now I was sweating up a storm. Jake wasn't even warm yet since he was still lying under the tree. I swear I thought I even saw him smiling at me.

I finely managed to rope the little donkey who luckily for me decided to stop running. I was thinking I had this situation under control now. The donkey led right up to the back of the trailer but he wouldn't go in for anything. By then I was really hot and sweaty and dirty from all the dust we'd stirred up. I tried and tried to get him in the trailer. Meanwhile, Jake moved over to a different tree in the shade so he could see me working with that donkey a little better. I think he was still laughing at me. I had taught Jake he couldn't work or bite horses so he was just lying back and watching like a good dog.

I finally got the little donkey lined up and almost in the trailer before he just planted all four feet and wouldn't budge. I'd been at this probably two hours by now and I was not going to give up - this donkey was going home with me one way or another.

It was at this point that I decided I had to get Jake's help and since this was only a little donkey and not really a horse I could bend the rules a little. I told Jake to "Walk up" which meant for him to go up to the stock. He walked right up behind that donkey like he knew exactly what I needed. I had the donkey all lined up at the trailer. When Jake got close I told him to "Watch him" a couple times then I gave the command, "Bite him". He gave that donkey a quick nip on the hind leg and it jumped right into the trailer! I was so happy to finally have that donkey in my trailer I could almost cry. I tied him in and quickly shut the trailer gate. As I bent down to pet Jake, who mind you, was barely even warm, the sweat ran down my face and into my eyes, darn near blinding me. I still managed to catch Jake looking at me with an expression that clearly said "If you would of asked me to help an hour ago we would of already been home."

Chapter 21

Could You Do That Again

2005

One summer in 2005 I wound up going to Reno, Nevada to participate in some roping events. While I happened to be there, enjoying my time away from home and cattle chores, I got a phone call from a neighbor. He started right off by asking, "Hey Marvin, do you have some steers missing?"

"Well, I don't know. I'm in Reno, Nevada." I replied.

"Oh…well, we have a bunch of steers up here. They're all spotted with long horns and I think they're yours."

"Hmmm….those do sound like my roping steers,"

"Well, they're at our house and we've got them in my little arena. What do you want me to do?"

"Since I'm in Reno right now there's not much I can do. I won't be home for a few days but…"

"That's fine," he cuts in. "They'll be okay until you get back. We'll keep them in the arena with food and water."

"Okay," I told him, "I sure appreciate it."

I came home a few days later and I could actually see my cattle at my neighbor's place as I drove by to get to my house. There they were, my roping steers, in a little 80 by 100 foot three-board arena! I figured I needed to go get them before they did some real property damage.

The minute I pulled into my driveway I backed up to the trailer, hooked it up, grabbed my dog Sport and headed over to the neighbor's. I didn't bring my horse because I was sure this would be a quick operation using my dogs! When I pulled into my neighbor's place I backed right up to the arena gate since he didn't have any pens or corrals to use for loading.

Normally I work these steers with my dogs all the time so they all knew the routine. I sent Sport out to fight with them for a little while and get their attention. Sport got them bunched up but I didn't have a lane to work them through, just that open gate so I figured we'd just do our best and try not to bust up any fence! I had Sport help me push them in the trailer and it went something like this; two would run in, then one would run out; three would run in then two would run out; and so on!

By then I had about five people outside watching me and Sport round these steers up out of this little arena. It took us about ten minutes to get them in the trailer but finally they were all in the trailer, the trailer gate was closed and I told Sport to lie down and take a break for a bit. We both were hot, tired, and sweaty. I was getting Sport some water when this lady who lived across the road, and who had been watching the whole thing, came over and said in the sweetest voice, "Could you unload them and do that again!"

"Sorry, but NO MA'AM," I laughed! "Me and my dog are way too tired so I think we'll just be going home. You know, I got lucky loading these steers without too much hassle and that's good enough for me!"

"Well I sure would like to watch that some more," she said, sweet as sugar.

"Well, it's probably not gonna happen today, ma'am!" I chuckled. It was like Sport was getting a standing ovation! But, that was enough show for one day!

Chapter 22
The Lone Tree In Montana
June 2005

In memory of my father-in-law, Jack Peasley.

As was typical for the summer time, my wife Jodi, our grown kids Laura and Jason and I were in Montana at my buddy Scott's ranch. On this trip Jodi's father, Jack, was also with us.

There happened to be this lone pine tree up on top of the mountain behind the cabins where we were staying. One evening Jason and I decided we were going to ride up there on our horses. We left with our bright yellow slickers on because it was just starting to rain. We had only gone about 50 feet from the cabin when the rain dumped buckets on us! We didn't care. We were just going to run up to this lone pine tree really quick for the fun of it! We took the dogs with us because they were always up for an adventure!

You know, I didn't realize how steep the mountain was or how far up that tree was! We rode for awhile before I finally said, "Jason, we're just not going to make it. Our horses can't handle this! It's way too steep."

We turned around and headed back down the mountain. But not wanting to head back to the cabins right then, we decided to ride in a different direction for a little while. We were walking our horses down this canyon when I heard this droning noise coming from above. It was getting really loud really quick. I glanced up and saw a fighter jet come screaming across the sky, almost out of nowhere, and heading right over us! I had my 60 foot rope with me and I almost think I could have roped that fighter jet he was so low! This all happened so quickly. I yelled, "Jason, get a hold of your horse." I grabbed onto my saddle horn because I figured these horses were going to flip out and kill us! The noise was so loud and the jet was so low that my dogs scattered underneath the nearest sage brush. The jet went racing by, turned up another canyon and went out of site. Of course you could hear it for a long time after it was gone.

Jason and I started laughing. Our horses hadn't even flinched! I thought they were going to flip out, bolt or do something crazy because that noise sure scared me half to death. It was terrible. As soon as we could call the dogs out from under the sagebrush and my blood pressure was back to normal, we rode back to the cabins.

Later, I asked Scott about the fighter jet.

"They ride through these canyons to do training when they're not supposed to, I think. They just cut up and down these canyons all the time." He told me.

That evening in the cabin Jodi and Jack asked me and Jason about the lone tree. I said, "We never made it. The mountain was too steep. I don't think anyone could make it up there!"

The next day Jason and I went sage rat hunting. About eight hours later we headed back to the cabin. When we arrived everyone was sitting around relaxing. After putting up my horse I walked in the cabin to change out of my hunting clothes when I noticed this little piece of pine tree limb lying on the table.

"No way!" I exclaimed loudly.

Jodi, Jack, and Laura could hear me from outside and they all started laughing. When I came back out to do my own relaxing, they showed me and Jason the pictures they took. The three of them had taken a ride up to the lone pine tree. However, they were smart enough to ride up another trail that was on the back side of that steep mountain. They went all the way around that mountain to find that trail! Then they took all kinds of pictures so I would see just how smart they were for finding their way up there!

And that little piece of pine tree bough that they brought back? Well, that was just to remind me how they had made it to the top!

One of the pictures they took that day is on the mantle in our house in Newberg, Oregon. It's a picture of Jodi and her dad next to that little lonesome pine tree.

Chapter 23
Just Point Me in the Right Direction
Summer 2005

I would have had a hard time believing this if I hadn't seen it for myself. My son Jason and I were at this guy's house and he was talking to us about cow dogs, "I had some cows out one time and my dog couldn't see them. I kept sending my dog out and he kept coming back to me without the cows. I could see the cows but I got to wondering. Well, the grass was pretty high by then and I thought maybe my dog can't see them. So I pick my dog up and point him at the cows. As soon as he sees them his head and tail go up! I set him right straight down on the ground and tell him to 'hunt them up'. He takes off and within minutes he brings the cows back!"

After we left I told my son, "You know of course that it's not nice to doubt people when they tell you a story, right? But I have to say that story was darn funny to listen to but kind of hard to believe." We had a good laugh over it and figured that was the end of that.

Two or three years later, Jason and I decided to go to Texas to check out some cow dogs. We arrived at this ranch and met this ol' boy named Jason also. I told him, "We'd like to see your dogs work some cows." He said no problem so we jumped in his truck and drove the four or five miles to where he had his cattle.

When we were a little distance from the cattle Jason gets his dogs down from the truck, whistled to get their attention, then sent them out to get the cows saying "Hunt them up". This one dog took off into sage brush that was higher than your belt! Pretty soon the dog comes back without the cows. Jason tells him two or three more times to go fetch up those cows but the dog still isn't coming back with any cows. Of course we can see the cows standing in the field a couple hundred yards from us.

Finally it dawns on Jason and he exclaims, "This dog can't see them!" I start laughing because I know what he's fixing to do. As he picked that dog up I looked at my son and my son looked at me and we're both doing our best not to burst out laughing. Jason pointed that dog around like a gun until he was looking straight at those cows. As soon as that dog caught sight of those cows his head and tail went straight up. Jason set him down, told him to fetch the cows and that dog took off like a shot! In less than five minutes he came back with the cows and brought them right up to the truck. By then my son Jason and I were laughing out loud real good.

I ended up buying a pup from that guy that very day. I couldn't have left without one of his dogs. I never would have imagined it was even possible to point a dog in the right direction let alone that it would work! I guess it makes sense when you think about it. I'd just never seen anything like that before!

Chapter 24
A Real Beach Trip
Fall 2005

A couple of buddies of mine from Montana, Scott and John, drove over to my place in Oregon in the fall of 2005 to pick up a horse. They were going to be in town for a few days so I asked them if they'd like to go ride horses on the beach at Pacific City. Since Montana doesn't have many beach riding opportunities, they were pretty jazzed to go!

My son and daughter, Jason and Laura, also wanted to go so we loaded up five good Quarter Horses; Badger, Comet, Bug, Pitch, and Himmie and headed out to Pacific City. It was going to be a regular beach party!

It was such a nice day to ride, with such a great group of people, and those Montana boys were sure enjoying the beach!

We'd been riding about an hour or so when I looked down the beach and saw a vehicle stuck in the sand. Pacific City is one of the few beaches in Oregon where you're allowed to drive your car onto the sand.

This poor guy was pushing on his car as hard as he could to get it out of the sand while his wife was gunning the engine. The car was not budging. All they were doing was creating deep ruts in the wake of flying sand! The guy was putting tree limbs and driftwood and whatever else he could find under the tires to try to get a little traction, but nothing was working.

Well if you know me you also know I never go riding without a rope on my saddle! I told the folks I was riding with that I thought we should help pull the car out of the sand. Laura laughed and asked, "You're not serious?"

I said, "Yes I am. I am darn serious! What are ropes and horses good for if you can't use them when you need them?"

We rode up to the couple and I asked them if they would mind if a couple horses pulled their vehicle out of the sand! "Sure," they said with disbelieving looks on their faces! "Do you really think you can do that?" I told the couple that we'd pull their vehicle out with our horses if they would let Scott drive. At this point they were agreeable to anything that might work.

Everyone was laughing by then because it really was a pretty comical situation! Scott, who was riding a colt of mine, got off his horse and behind the wheel to do the driving. Luckily Jason was riding his horse Comet. That was a horse that didn't have any quit in him and would pull whatever he was hooked up to. I was riding my horse Badger and he was basically the same; hook him up to something and he wouldn't stop pulling until you made him quit.

Everyone got out of the way and Scott hooked mine and Jason's rope to the vehicle. We tightened our ropes and Scott got into the vehicle and said he was ready. Comet and Badger started pulling and Scott helped by doing a little pushing himself from the driver's side!

By this time we had an audience. It is not very often people get to witness horses pulling a vehicle out of the sand!

We pulled until we had that vehicle out of the sand and on to solid ground! Needless to say the couple, who happened to be visiting from Florida, were darn happy and although everyone was laughing, no one was laughing at me anymore!

When we were riding off I mentioned how great it would have been to have taken some pictures. My friend John piped-up and said he had taken a camera full of pictures! That just made my day. I couldn't wait to get home and see how they turned out!

When I finally saw the pictures, I got the last laugh. I knew we sent that couple from Florida home with a memory from Oregon they will never forget! I hope someday they'll get to see those pictures too!

Chapter 25
Calves as Wild as March Hares
March 2006

It seems like when people buy calves they either buy two or three. Well this guy named Keith bought three big calves and they had escaped. He called me in a panic, "Hey, I've got some calves out and I hear you're the guy to catch them."

"I'll sure be glad to try," I told him.

"They're wild as March Hares," he warned, "But we know where they are; they're lying out in the middle of this big ol' field."

"Good," I said, "It makes it a lot easier for us to get them if we know where they are." I called my brother-in-law, John and asked him if he wanted to help. "Sure," he said. He always thought it was fun to go out with me and see what kind of trouble I got into. I asked my son Jason and of course he wanted to help.

We went to saddle up our horses and pull the dogs, Bob and Sport, from their kennels. Then we loaded everyone up and met John in town. John brought his daughter, Brandi, with him and a four-wheeler instead of horses.

When we arrived at Keith's house he came running out to meet us, "Hey! Thanks for coming! Those calves are right down the road here and they're lying in a big ol' field."

Jason and I drove to where Keith directed us. The gravel road we were on was at the top of a hill and we could see the calves below us in the field. They were starting to get up just from hearing the sound of our trucks and we were still three or four hundred yards away. "Man Jason, this is going to be a fight." One look at those jumpy calves and I knew this wasn't going to be easy.

"Yea, it sure looks like it," he agreed.

We parked next to John on the gravel road and as we were getting out I said, "Man, these things are wild; they're Limousin calves." Keith had just come walking up when I asked him, "How'd they get out?"

"I unloaded them out of my trailer and they didn't even slow down. They just tore down the corral and left." Well now I knew how wild they were! We rode down to where the calves were and tried to gather them up. This turned into a lot of running around with nothing good coming from it. I rode up next to Jason, "You know what; we just have to get a rope on them and get them stopped. We're not going to be able to herd them anywhere!"

By now the calves were going in three different directions. This just made it really tough. The dogs couldn't seem to get them stopped either. They were biting and chewing on them but those calves were just running through them like they weren't even there. I went after this one big calf which must have weighed over 800 pounds when he made a run for the creek bed. I ran up close to him on my horse and threw my rope. The loop I threw was a bit big and the calf was running through it as I was dallying it on my horn. I turned my horse to the left, took up the slack, and actually ended up with the calf's back leg in my rope. I jerked the calf down to the ground.

John and Brandi raced up on the four-wheeler. They jumped off and held the calf's head down while I got a rope around his neck. I led the calf over to the trailer with John and Brandi's help but it still took the three of us a half hour of fighting to get him inside the trailer.

"Does anybody have any idea where the other two went?" I asked, trying to catch my breath.

"Yeah, they're in the brush down there in the corner." John pointed in the direction of the other two.

Just as Jason rode up to us on his horse I said to him, "Jason, let's go down there and see if we can get them out." We loped over to the other calves with our dogs following along. I sent the dogs in the brush to get the two calves out of that corner and sure enough they bolted out and took off in two different directions. I hollered at Jason, "We better take the one heading for town!" We were chasing that calf as it cut through people's yards, ran back across the fields, then through some more private property and finally towards a big field. If it made it across the big field it would be on the main road at the edge of town. Not really a good place for that wild calf to be!

My horse couldn't catch up with him so I yelled over to Jason, "See if you can get ahead of him and get him stopped." He ran his horse up in front of the calf, got him to stop then tried to rope him. It didn't work. But he did get him turned and the calf headed back the opposite way. The dogs managed to slow him enough that I was able to throw a rope on him and pull him to a stop.

By this time Jason and I were sweating, the dogs were panting and the calf was hot. "Let's get him back to the trailer and load him up."

Jason and I with the help of the dogs got this calf back to the trailer which was about three quarters of a mile away. John and Brandi were waiting for us and it took all four of us to load him in the trailer.

"Now," I asked, "where's the last one?" John pointed and I could see the calf in the brush over in a corner. I decided before we attempted to catch this last calf we were going to take a break, water the dogs, and let the horses cool off.

After a bit of rest and some thinking, I said to Jason, "Let's set up so both sides of that corner are blocked. That way when he comes out of there one of us can get a rope on him."

We sent the dogs to bring the calf out. As he came out of the brush Jason got a rope on him and dallied off to his horn. I threw another rope on him because I had a bigger horse and that way I knew there was no way he was breaking free. Between me and Jason we led him back to the trailer. Keith was there by the trailers waiting for us. I noticed a bunch of people on the top of the hill watching us.

"What's going on?" I asked. "Who are all those people up there watching us?"

"I don't know. I don't know half of them," Keith said. "But the word is out you're here and everybody wants to come watch what you do for fun." He paused then added, "…but this doesn't look like much fun to me!"

"Man, we love it." I told him. "It's just a nice way to spend time with family and friends!"

Once the last calf was in the trailer we drove them over to Keith's house and put them in a strong round corral with high-sided panels. I gave him a little friendly cow advice, "Keith, how about you keep these calves in here for a while. Feed them and try to gentle them down a little before you let them out in those big fields again."

"Oh man, they're not going in the field for awhile!" he groaned. I just laughed and told him I'd come and catch them again if need be!

Once we loaded everything up Keith asked, "What do I owe you."

"Oh…I don't know. How about since it's such a hot day and all you just give us enough for the four of us to go to Dairy Queen for some ice cream. That'll work for me."

He gave me a fifty dollar bill and we took off for the Dairy Queen. Over burgers and ice cream we talked about the day and what a great adventure we had. Those are the kinds of memories I like to look back on over and over again. It was just good ol' cowboy fun that day!

Chapter 26
Three Lost Calves in Dayton, Oregon
August 2006

One day while driving to a fencing job I got a phone call. Since I didn't have my headset on I figured I'd just let it go to voicemail then pull over when I had a chance to listen to it. Well, that was a bad idea since I had to sit and listen to a 20 minute long voice message from a guy telling me about his loose cattle. And like anybody who has loose cattle, he needed to catch them right away. Of course in his case they were out on the highway in Dayton, Oregon. So as you can imagine he sounded pretty frantic. In his message he told me how he bought three calves, brought them home and they immediately escaped. He couldn't do anything with them. They were wild renegades that had run off!

It was Friday afternoon and I already had plans with my son, Jason. We were going Jack Pot Roping. He was determined to win himself a little bit of money that he could put in the bank. He was saving it so that when he got old enough he could buy a pickup truck. Our deal was I would pay the entry fees if he didn't win and he would pay the entry fees if he did win! Either way, it was a good deal for him.

I called the guy with the loose calves back. He told me over and over, "I have to catch them now." He wanted me to do it and he wouldn't take no for an answer. I told him what it would cost for me to go home and get everything loaded up; the dogs; the horses; and the gear. I also knew I was probably going to have to talk my son out of going roping so he could help me out.

We came to an agreement on the cost. I don't think at that point money was even an issue for him. He just wanted his cows off the highway!

When I arrived home I found Jason and explained the situation.

"I really wanted to go roping." Jason said.

"Well, we're guaranteed money if we go catch his calves. He has to pay us just to show up. If we're successful he'll pay us even more and I'll split it with you."

Jason didn't even have to think twice about this because it was a sure money deal. "Well, let's go catch some calves then!"

We got my horse Badger and Jason's horse Comet ready. We decided to only take the one dog, Sport, with us. We got the trailer hooked up, the truck loaded, and everything was ready to go.

We drove to Dayton and found the guy. His mother was with him and he was a nervous wreck. He said, "Man, I don't know what I'm going do. I have to catch my calves. There's a huge nursery up the road. If they get in there I'm going to get sued; if they get hit by a car I'm going to get sued."

He continued on and on until I finally interrupted him and asked, "Well sir, where are they?"

"I'm not sure," he said.

"Where were they seen last?"

He took us down the road and showed us where he'd last seen them. There was a newly planted filbert orchard and the trees were not even two feet tall yet. He pointed and said, "They went across this orchard and to the left."

"All right. We'll ride out and look." Jason and I cinched our saddles up, called for Sport and rode out.

"I think they're in that big filbert orchard over across the way" I said to Jason as we rode out. The guy told us they'd gone in the opposite direction but I just had a feeling he was wrong.

Jason and I rode all over looking for the cattle. We rode for maybe an hour and we couldn't find anything, not even any tracks. It was summer and the ground was really too dry to show any tracks. Finally Jason got off his horse so he could be closer to the ground and started looking for tracks. "Hey! Here's a track, right here." He exclaimed. The track was headed the way I thought they had gone - into the big filbert orchard.

"We have a problem. There are two of us, two horses, two ropes, one dog and three steers! There is no way we can rope all three!" I didn't like the way this was heading. By then we were a mile or two from the truck and it was just too far to try and get three calves back to it. I turned to Jason and said, "Let's go get our truck and bring it over here. I'm sure the cattle are in those filberts." We rode back to the truck then drove it closer, parking on the edge of the big filbert orchard.

We started riding again and sure enough we found the calves in the middle of the big filbert orchard. I said to Jason, "Let's get around them...we really need to keep them out of the nursery on the other side of this orchard."

There was only one strand of hot wire fence between the orchard and the nursery and this was a big, nice nursery, it was going to be important to keep them out of there. I rode out of the orchard to talk to the guy who owned the calves. I said, "Here's our plan. We're going to try to push them out here across the road and into this new filbert orchard. I'm going to see if my dog can bay them up and hold them in these blackberries. You watch the traffic and we'll get them coming this way. Make sure you block the road and don't let a car hit them!"

We went back with the dog and the horses and got behind the calves and headed them the right way. They almost got to the road when they stopped, turned around and went back into the big filbert orchard! We tried again and after about the third or fourth time they took off and this time were headed straight towards the nursery!

I was tired, hot, and unhappy! I sent Sport into the orchard and told him to "get ahead". We couldn't see Sport but we could hear him barking and a calf bawling. "Well, if they're fighting he's got them stopped!" I told Jason. I looked through the filberts and sure enough, he had them balled up out in the big filbert orchard! I said, "Let's ride around behind them now and see if we can call the dog off and push the calves out." That's what we did. I hollered at the guy who owned them, "Hey, make sure you block the road because we're going bring them out in the middle of it."

As soon as Sport backed off those calves we were able to push them out of the orchard. Once they started trotting I told Sport to "Get up there" and "Bay 'em up".

Of course, I was getting more confident with the situation because I knew Sport would ball them up. I told Jason, "That big calf is the one I want to rope!"

We finally got the cows across the road. Then we headed them into the trees next to a blackberry patch that ran alongside the orchard and held them there.

I asked the man who owned them, "Hey, can you drive a truck and trailer?"

"Yeah, a little bit."

I'm thinking to myself, 'Oh man! There's no way I'm gonna be able to leave these cows alone with Sport to drive that truck and trailer!' So I hollered back to the guy, "Well, give her a try. All you have to do is back straight up. Just put one side against the blackberry patch then open the trailer gate and we'll see if we can get the cattle in the trailer."

He backed up the truck and trailer but he was going back too far and Jason and I started screaming at him to stop. He finally stopped when he hit the blackberry bushes! I told Jason, "When he gets that gate open, you stay back here and wait for the cattle and keep them from running off the back side. I'll hold the trailer gate open and have Sport bring them to me." By then the calves were whipped and didn't want to run much anymore. I rode up and the guy opened the trailer gate. I held it open and had Sport "Bring 'em" to me and just like that they walked right up to the trailer! I thought, well that was easy!

I thought "easy" too soon. Right when the ring leader was about to step into the trailer he stopped, turned and charged my dog. Sport wasn't going to have any of that! He grabbed him right by the nose and the calf bawled, stopped and turned for the trailer. I thought, man, we've got him now!

By now the other two calves had jumped into the trailer but the big one stopped again, turned around and tried to stare down my dog!

Luckily Sport was well trained and knew how to be patient. He stood there and let the calf walk towards him. As soon as the calf got about a foot from him I said "Bite" and he grabbed that calf right on the nose again! The calf turned and started into the trailer. Sport went to lay down just as that calf stopped and turned around again. I thought, *'Oh, no, not again!'* He charged my dog for the second time and once again Sport grabbed him by the nose! This calf just did not want to give up!

Jason was nearby ready to help but he was laughing so hard he practically fell of his horse! Of course the guy who owned the calves was laughing too by then. To him it looked like we had it under control. Now it was starting to be fun for him!

The calf turned and started for the trailer and Sport lay down again. The calf put a foot in the trailer and then he stopped, backed up, turned around and walked square up to my dog like he was going to stomp him like a coyote! I told Sport "Bite him" and he grabbed him by the nose for the fourth time and that calf turned around and promptly went into the trailer. The funniest thing was those other two calves in the trailer watching this unfold. They just stayed right inside that trailer; they didn't want anything to do with Sport!

The moment that last ornery calf jumped into the trailer I slammed the trailer gate shut. That little calf and dog battle had probably only taken five minutes but it seemed like five hours.

As soon as I got off my horse the owner ran up and started shaking my hand. "Thank you, thank you", over and over again was all he could say!

Now that the calves were secure I stepped down from my horse and called Sport over to me. I gave him some good scratches behind the ears to let him know he was a good dog. And boy, that day, as was most days with Sport, he had done an exceptional job!

I shut the divider so the calves were in the front section then I loaded up my horse in the back part of the trailer. I got Sport back up into the truck and chained him securely so he wouldn't fall out.

The guy's mom had been sitting out in a car in the middle of the road the whole time watching all this. I walked over to her. She looked up at me from her car window and said, "My gosh, I've never seen the likes. I can't believe what I just saw."

"Well ma'am, don't go around telling people what you just saw. They're not going to believe you. They're going to think you need help!" She started laughing. She thought that was pretty funny.

We followed the guy and his mom back to their house in my truck and trailer, unloaded the calves and put them in the corral. As we were getting ready to head out the guy says to me, "You know what? I lost two calves about a year ago down on the river bottom. I've never seen them but I hear rumors of them once in a while". I looked over at Jason and said, "You want to go down to the river bottom and see if we can find those two calves."

"Yeah, let's do it!"

The guy took us down to the spot where he had last heard of a sighting. There were thousands of acres of pastures and swamp and a big, long, winding river bottom.

We unloaded the horses, cinched up the saddles and started looking for the cattle. We rode for a couple hours but we never saw anything; not a cow track, cow dung, nothing. Finally we had to give up because it was starting to get dark. I told Jason, "We need to load up and go home." I called the guy and told him we couldn't find them. I did add, "If you hear rumors of them again, give us a call."

Jason and I talked about how fun it would be and a dream come true to find calves lost in hundreds and hundreds of acres! Unfortunately it was a dream that just wasn't going to come true that day! I never did hear from that guy again so I guess he never saw or heard rumor of his other two calves.

Chapter 27
Catching Calves for Max
Summer 2006

I went down to the local Wilco Farm Store one day to pick up fence supplies when I saw this guy I know run out of the store. I know him because he works there and I know for a fact he hardly ever runs. But today he was in a big hurry trotting across the parking lot so I hollered out, "Hey, Max…where you going?"

"Oh, hey there Marvin! Somebody spotted my calves and I'm gonna go try and get 'em."

"So you have some loose, huh?"

"Yeah, there're two of them. We've been after them for a week or two and can't catch them."

I pried a little more of the story out of him before he got in his truck. According to him they had chased those two calves on horses, on four-wheelers, and on foot, run them through a couple fences and everything else until they finally lost them!

"Well" I said, "if you need any help let me know and I'll come and catch them." I went inside and got what I needed and left.

A day or two later I was heading into Wilco again when here comes Max, trotting out across the parking lot. "Max, you still after them calves?"

"Yeah, they've been spotted."

"Man if you want I'll be glad to catch them for you."

"Naw," he puffs as he hustles by, "we'll get them…we'll get them this time."

"Okay. Well give me a call if you need some help."

That night about eight or nine o'clock the phone rang and it was Max. "Hey are you serious about helping me catch those calves?"

"Well sure man, that's what I do for a hobby you know - catch cattle."

He explains, "Man, their wild as deer."

"I'll be glad to catch them. What happened?"

"I bought them…there's three of them…bought them at the sale barn and brought them home and put 'em in the corral. They just went in there, tore it down and left! We caught one but we can't catch the other two.

We've had people down here with horses…and ropes…and four-wheelers and they just won't get caught."

"Well how about I come and get them tomorrow."

"Ah, you know, that'd be great!"

I hung up the phone and called a buddy of mine, Josh. "You up for catching a couple of calves tomorrow?" I asked him.

"Sure. Where?"

"Just meet at my house," I told him. "I've got the dogs, the horses, the ropes; everything we'll need."

The next day Josh met me and we saddled up my horse Badger and my daughter's horse, Bug, for Josh to ride. I pulled my dogs Sport and Chic from their kennels and put them in their dog boxes on the truck. We loaded up the horses and drove to meet Max down on the Willamette river bottom.

Once we got there and unloaded I asked where the calves were. "I'm not sure," Max said. "I think they're on this property up in the woods."

"We'll go get them, Max, don't you worry." I reassured him.

"Well," he asked, "What do you want me to do?"

"How about you hang out until I need you? I'll let you know. I'll get my dogs to bay them up then we'll rope them. Just bring you're trailer down here and we'll load them out in the field."

"You're going to load them out in the field?" He seemed surprised with this.

"Well, we don't have any corrals so it's about the only choice we have."

"Really? It's just that easy?" I can see some doubt flicker across his face.

"Well I don't know. I'll tell you when we get it done!" I laughed.

Max knew how hard it is to catch cattle because he'd been trying to do it for a lot of days with no success. I think that was why he was a bit surprised at how easy I was making it sound. But if I have some good dogs with me it can often make the difference between catching the cattle in one day versus a week.

Josh and I took off where Max thought those calves would be. Pretty soon Josh asked me, "What's your plan?"

"Well," I told him, "if we find these calves in these woods we have to get them out and head them for that field. I'll sic the dogs on them and we'll just bay them up in that field and put a rope on them."

"All right!"

We rode around in the woods for about ten minutes. It wasn't a very big piece of property, about 30 acres or so. We finally spotted them.

"Let's move around the back side of them and head them out in that field." We rode around and I called my dogs along with me. I kept my dogs by my horse and Josh and I pushed them out in the field just using our horses.

I always try to time it so my dogs can get after the cattle quickly - particularly when they get in a field. Unless it's a mowed hay field, the grass is usually so high it's easy for them to get away from us.

The cattle started out across the field and I turned the dogs loose on them. Sport and Chic took off and quickly got the calves bayed up in the middle of the field. As Josh and I were riding out there I told him, "I'll go for the first one, he's the biggest. You get the second one." We were about 20 feet from them and they weren't paying much mind to us because there were already two dogs bothering them. Every time they tried to run off a dog grabbed them on the nose and forced them back together and in one spot.

When I had a chance I roped the biggest one but no sooner had I pulled back on my slack when he charged into the side of my horse! The other calf was trying to get away so I set the dogs on him. Of course everything was going crazy by then. Josh got a rope on the other calf and yelled over to me, "What do you want me to do now?"

"Let's just head them that a ways." I pointed. We had to take them three or four hundred yards farther to even get them to a truck and trailer.

The dogs were pretty good about bringing them along. I started toward the trailer and the dogs got behind my calf to help encourage him along. Josh's calf, of course, wanted to follow the calf I was leading. We got to moving through that field pretty good when I started hollering at Max to get his truck and trailer ready because he was just standing there having a good ol' time watching us!

He snapped out of it and ran to get his truck and trailer parked out in the field. We came up closer and he was hollering to me asking what he was supposed to do.

"Just stay back, Max...no telling how mad these calves are going to get" I hollered. "Can you just hold the trailer gate open? We'll see if we can get them in there."

I kept fighting my calf because he was a mean one but I managed to pull him around so the dogs could get him lined up to the trailer. It took the dogs about five minutes to get him in the trailer. I told Max to shut the divider until I could tie him towards the front of the trailer. Once he was secured we opened the divider back up so the other calf could see him. If the other calf could see his buddy it'd be easier to get him to go into the trailer. Josh got around with his calf and the dogs helped line him up to the trailer. Pretty soon that little calf sees the other one in the trailer and he shoots inside really quick! We wasted no time shutting the door!

Max was just standing there looking a little amazed. "Man, I can't believe how easy you made that look using the dogs!"

Like he'd told me, they'd been after those calves for something like two weeks; running around out there with horses and ropes and four-wheelers and having no luck whatsoever. It took me and my dogs less than a couple hours to get the job done!

The big secret about catching cows successfully is getting them stopped. That can be hard without dogs. My dogs can usually get them stopped nine times out of ten and that's why having cow dogs gives me an advantage when I'm catching cattle. And that's why Max got his calves back!

Chapter 28
You Don't Like the Sound of My Voice?
Summer 2006

One summer I bought a Hangin' Tree Cowdog named Tree from Scott, a buddy of mine who lives in Montana, and brought him home to Oregon. I tried and tried to work this dog but he just wouldn't work for me. I knew he was a good working dog because I had seen him work on Scott's ranch before. So I called Scott up one day and told him, "This dog won't work for me."

"I don't understand," he replied. "Just keep him with you for awhile longer and see if that makes a difference."

Everywhere I went I took that dog with me. I did that for three months and he still wouldn't work for me anymore than the day I first got him.

I called Scott again and he told me to bring him back, he'd return my money.

Eventually I had some time to drive back to Montana with Tree. When I got to Scott's ranch he promptly told me, "I just don't understand that dog; he'll work for me."

"I know. I saw him work with you." I lamented but I was also thinking maybe it was because Scott had raised Tree from a pup and he was just super bonded to him.

We decided to go out cruising across the ranch in Scott's truck. At one point while we were out driving we spotted several head of cows about four hundred yards away. I pointed to the cows and said to Scott, "Let's stop. You turn Tree loose and let's see if he goes to work."

Scott let Tree out and I stayed in the truck. He pointed Tree in the right direction and gave him a common command, one that's typically used with any cow dog, and that dog had those cows back to the truck in no time! I was stunned! I just shook my head and told him, "Man that dog won't work for anybody but you! I don't understand that."

Six months later Scott called me. We were doing a little talking about this and that when I finally asked him, "What did you ever do with your dog Tree."

He said, "I sold him to a guy in Utah." I knew this Utah guy because I had sold dogs to him too. "Is he working for that guy?"

"Yeah," he said. "Tree is doing great!"

I just scratched my head over this. But what the heck, guess it was just one of those weird deals.

Several months later I talked to Scott again and right away he said, "I got Tree back."

"How come," I asked?

"Well, he wouldn't work for that guy either. He would work with his son but once the son went back to school, Tree quit working."

"Is he working for you?"

"Yeah, he's working for me."

We talked a bit more then made some plans to work dogs again once the weather got better. I kept thinking about that dog though. It really is strange to see a dog act like that. Somehow it seemed that this dog wouldn't work for anybody but Scott and the Utah guy's son. Strange indeed!

It was some time later but eventually I drove back to Montana to work cows with Scott. I had brought Sport along with me and he had Tree. We happened to be out in the field when about 200 cows busted through this gate. Scott told Tree to "Go get 'em" but the dog wouldn't leave. He stayed by the side of Scott's horse and wouldn't work! So I sent Sport out instead. Poor Sport hadn't seen that many cows in his life! He got them stopped though and even brought them back. I got to thinking once we had those cows settled. "You know what Scott? I think your dog will work if I'm not by him! I think that as soon as he hears me talking he quits working."

Scott started to protest but I cut him off, "Let's try this. I'm going to ride off and get a ways away from you. You start working Tree and see if he'll work." I rode off three or four hundred yards then Scott instructed Tree to go to work. Sure enough, that dog went to work!

As soon as I rode back up to Scott and started talking, his dog stopped working!

To this day I don't know why that happened. I can't explain it other than Tree must not have liked the sound of my voice. I have never had that experience before or since. I guess I just didn't sound like anybody that dog wanted to hear!

Chapter 29
Sport and Matt's Loose Cattle
November 2006

Everyone around my home town of Newberg Oregon knew my dog Sport and his amazing ability as a cow dog. I can take some credit because I trained him but he was also bred to be a cow dog with great instinct and abilities. I was also lucky because he was especially talented and good at what he did!

It so happens that I work with cow dogs and cattle gathering as a hobby but earn my living building fences. I have a fence building business called Marvin's Fencing. One day Matt, a man I had built a fence for, called me and said, "Hey Marvin, my cows are out. I forgot to close the gate this morning and they're over at my neighbor's house with his cows. I've got to get them home. Can you help?"

"Well…" I hesitated. I happened to be standing by the window watching the sun go down, "…it's almost dark."

"That's all right. Bring Sport, he can do it!" Matt sure had a lot of confidence in my dog!

"Naw, I'm not bringing Sport over. And really…it's just too dark!" I had my reasons! I knew Matt's cattle setup. We were going to have to bring these cows down two roads with a horse and a dog and no trailers because the property they were on didn't have any corrals. I wasn't about to do that in the dark.

I asked, "So, how many cattle are over there?"

Matt said, "I've got five and the neighbor has ten or fifteen."

"Let's do it first thing in the morning." I told him then added, "Before I start work. I'll just bring my horse and Sport and the guy who works for me can bring the four-wheeler." Fortunately Matt's house and property was three miles away from mine, all on gravel roads.

The next morning my helper, Jared, showed up thinking we were going to go do our "planned" fence job. He was a little surprised when I told him our new plans, "Guess what? We have to go catch cows right now!"

"Catch cows?"

"Yup! I'll take the horse and dog and you take the four-wheeler." Of course Jared was jazzed up about this because I'm sure it sounded like a lot more fun than building fences!

I got everything ready and loaded up and we drove over to Matt's house. The cows were down in the neighbor's property surrounded by a rickety, falling-down fence. I thought we could get Matt's calves sorted out easily enough because they weren't mixing really well with the other herd in the field. It always takes awhile for new cows to get used to each other and mix in with another herd.

I rode in on my horse with Sport at my side and we got Matt's calves off to one side. Jared was a little way off on the four-wheeler so I hollered out to him, "You go up and block the road to the right. Don't let these calves get by you! Get them stopped if you can." Jared gave me a 'thumbs up'. He seemed to be having a lot more fun driving that four-wheeler around instead of building fence!

Matt was standing a little ways off. "What're you going to do Marvin?" He called out to me.

"I'm just going take these calves out the driveway to the road and I'm going turn them with my dog. When they hit the next road a couple hundred yards down I'm going have my dog turn them and put them back up on the main road. Then I'll have my dog go around them and turn them up the driveway." It sounded complicated even to me!

Matt was all enthusiasm though, "Sport can do it, man! He can do it!"

Jared took off to block his road and I went to move the calves out of the field. The calves were fighting a little bit but luckily for me they'd been worked by a dog at one time or another. I knew that because I'd owned some of them before I sold them to Matt.

Sport quickly got those calves out on the road from the field. Jared was positioned up the road a ways and ready to help turn them. Sport ran around the group, turned them the right way and moved them up to the next tee in the road. Matt was back with me by then just having a good ol' time watching this unravel. Since the calves were doing what they were supposed to do, Jared came back and was now driving alongside the calves on the four-wheeler. They started up Leander Road and only had to go a couple hundred yards to get to Matt's driveway. Now all of a sudden Matt was getting a little nervous. He was afraid Sport wouldn't be able to turn them up his driveway because he kept asking me when I was going to send

Sport in to start turning them. I explained to him there was no sense in do-ing that until the calves got closer to the turn.

Once the calves reached Matt's driveway I sent Sport around to the right side of them. Matt suddenly started yelling, "Don't let them get in the yard." His yard was at the end of the road we were on and he was worried the cattle were going to shoot past the driveway to his pasture, run into his nice yard and destroy it. While Matt was worrying, Sport circled around the calves, which is what a cattle dog is trained to do, and turned them left up the driveway to the pasture. He then drove them through the open gate into the pasture just as I had planned and I shut the gate when the last cow went through. With a sigh of relief Matt said, "Man, this was just so fun to watch…except for the part when they got near my yard!"

I laughed and told him, "Well now you know, just remember to shut the gate after you feed them in the morning or your nice yard might be the next place they run off to!"

"Oh, right! Don't worry…I will."

I told Matt it was time for me and Jared to get back to the fencing job so we say our good-byes. Jared and I rode back to the truck, him on the four-wheeler and me on my horse. Jared told me on the way back that it was just about the coolest thing he'd ever seen. He had never seen my dogs work cattle in a real-life situation. He'd only seen them work in the roping arena.

When you get your dogs out in real-life situations it's a whole different story than just working them on cattle in an arena. There is a lot more risk and you have to be careful of so many other hazards out there! There are roads with cars speeding by, kids out playing, people stopping to watch, other animals, nice fences and yards and difficult terrain. But even so, it sure is fun to get out and gather cattle, especially when I know I've saved someone a lot of grief and stress from having their cattle running loose. And of course it's always really neat when people are impressed with how amazing my dog Sport is!

Chapter 30
The Fog
Winter 2007

I was talking to my friend, Pat, one day about roping and cow dogs and he told me he had a neighbor, Bob, who had lost some calves in the mountains behind his house. I asked him how many and he told me two. He asked if I wanted to help him look for Bob's calves and of course I was all for that! We made arrangements to find those calves the upcoming weekend.

Later that day I asked my son Jason if he wanted to come along and he said he wouldn't miss it! My wife Jodi also wanted to come along.

Come Saturday morning we woke up to one of the wettest, foggiest days we'd had in a long time. The fog was so thick that you could hardly see five yards in front of you. I had a feeling this might prove to be a challenging day! But, we said we'd help and that's what we were going to do so we saddled our horses, hooked up the trailer and loaded them inside. I got Sport and Chic out from their kennels and put them in the dog boxes in the bed of my truck instead of putting them in the trailer because the weather was so nasty and cold, probably about the mid thirties. At least they'd stay dry and warm on the drive over to Pat's place!

We decided to stop and have some breakfast because we had no idea how long we would be riding and some hot food sounded nice on that cold morning. Once we finished eating we headed on down the road to the place we said we'd meet up with Pat. He and his wife were there waiting for us. We asked him if anyone had seen the calves to which he replied no. Both he and his wife were saddled up and ready to ride so we headed out from his place on horseback.

Before we started up into the mountains we needed to put our big yellow slickers on as it was misting rain. We made quite a sight in those slickers – I think you could have spotted us a couple miles away, even through the fog!

I asked Pat what the calves looked like and he gave me a general description. We rode and rode for hours in that foggy, wet weather without seeing anything, not even a deer. Eventually we rode by some property that belonged to a guy who happened to be a neighbor of Bob. I was looking in this guy's corals at his cattle when I saw a couple of calves that fit the description Pat gave me. I pointed them out to Pat saying they sure looked like the two calves he described. He agreed and went up to this guy's house to ask about the calves. The guy said they were all his cattle. So we kept riding until we got to a gravel road then we headed back a few miles to the trailer, never having spotted the missing calves.

"You know Pat," I said, "I don't think there's any need to look any more for those two calves."

"Why's that Marvin?" He asked me.

"Because those two calves are right there in that other guy's corral!" I had no doubt about this.

Jason, Jodi and I loaded up the horses and dogs, said our good-byes and left. Once we were on the road I told Jason, "I am almost 100% positive those two calves in the neighbor's corral belong to Bob." Jason thought so too based on the description Pat gave us of the calves.

It was maybe two days later when I got a call from Pat. He told me I was right, those two calves in the other guy's corrals were Bob's! He said it took a little convincing but Bob got them back and all was good now. I told him that was great news and we had a really nice ride anyway. We got to ride some new mountain roads and trails, even if we couldn't see them most of the time!

Chapter 31
Jennifer's Cows
August 2007

I met this lady, Jennifer, one summer when my brother-in-law and I went to her house to buy some cattle. After that I started building fence for her and her company. During one of those fence building projects, she told me she had cattle out at her dad's place and every year they had a heck of a time rounding them up. They were on 20 or 30 acres and there were only 11 cow-calf pairs and a bull but they sure were trouble. I told her, "I'd be glad to go catch them for you anytime you like. Just let me know."

It was about a year later when Jennifer and I talked about those cows again. She had to go out and get the cows because the grass was grazed down. I told her I would be glad to help but she said she and her dad could do it.

"Well if you need any help, let me know."

A few days later I got a call from her. "Would you mind catching those cattle for me?" She and her Dad were not having a good time trying to catch their cows! I told her I would be glad to help. I got a hold of Jason and we set up a date on the weekend to catch them. It seems like every time it gets close to when I've got to go gather a bunch of cattle I wake up three or four times in the night thinking about what all can go wrong! I've been lucky most of the time in the past with gathering other people's cattle so I just don't know why I do all that worrying. Other than the fact that it's dangerous business gathering cattle and I always want things to go off without a hitch.

Jason and I were saddling up our horses Comet and Badger the next morning when I warned him, "I'm not sure what we're getting into but I know these cows are snotty and mean because I bought some calves from her and they grew up to be that way! When we get out there we need to be careful!" We took my dogs, Sport and Bob, with us. My dog Bob was tough and ornery. He would lick a person to death but he thought cattle were just hamburger for him to eat!

We met up with Jennifer and her Dad and she had us follow them out to where the cattle were. The pens were set in the worse place possible –

along the side of the fence instead of in the corner. We run into this all the time when we're out gathering cattle. Normally it's because you can't get to the corner because of where the fields are located. Trees, creeks, brush or whatever, is usually in the way.

I had a 20 foot stock trailer with me and Jennifer had a truck and trailer too. "I think we should set up like this," she said and started explaining how the trucks, trailers and cattle panels needed to be. Then I told her the way I thought we should set up. When you gather cattle as much as I do you learn a thing or two. I felt the way she wanted me to set up the equipment and trailers was a no-win situation for my dogs. To be diplomatic I said, "Let's try it my way and if that doesn't work we'll regroup and set it up your way." Since I was the one with the dogs and the horses doing the hard work, I won out.

We parked our trucks and trailers in the field and set up the panels where I wanted them. I arranged it so all we had to do when we got the cattle in the paneled area was load them in trailers. We wouldn't have to move anything else.

Jennifer's Dad asked, "Marvin, what's your plan."

"I'll tell you what," I started. "It's hot and my dogs are not in the greatest shape because I've been busy building fence and don't get to work with them every day. So I think what we're going to do is this: Jason and I will ride out with the dogs and let them ball up the cows and beat them up a little bit to show them we're boss. Then I'll call my dogs off and let them go jump in the pond to cool off. We'll let our horses rest and then go back and ball them up again and put them in the corral."

"It's that easy?"

"I don't know. I tell people all the time 'when I'm done, I'll tell you if it was easy or not'! Right now that's our plan." That got a good chuckle out of everyone!

Jason and I rode out across the field with Bob and Sport. As we were riding toward the cows I said, "Jason, when we get over there these cows are going to come out and they're going to try and kill my dogs! So the first thing the dog has to do is whip them. We're gonna ball them up, get behind them and get them headed behind the trailer and the corrals. Anytime they get out of a walk I'm gonna send the dogs ahead to stop them and get them balled up. Then I'll just pull the dogs back and let 'em keep walking."

What most people don't know or understand about cow dogs is how rough the cattle situations can be for them. The job I was doing for Jennifer consisted of using my two dogs, along with some help from me and Jason, to put these cows in a corral, get them loaded in a trailer and take them back to their home. The way I work cows in a situation like this is different than if I were going out to dog break them. If I were going to dog break them I would hold them up and call my dogs off then go back the next day and do it again. I would do that for several days until they were respectful of the dogs and obedient about getting into the pens and trailer. By doing it this way, slowly over time, there was less chance for my dogs to get hurt because they were tired.

Jason and I rode our horses towards the cows. I had sent Sport and Bob ahead to get them stopped. First thing that happened was one of the cows peeled away from the group and was snot-blowing mad. She was going to kill Bob because he was the first one near her. She charged him but Bob was quicker and he chomped down on her ear hard! We never saw that cow again! Her head stayed in the herd the rest of the time! She didn't want anything else to do with my dog.

We ended up getting the cattle balled up without too much trouble. I called my dogs off and told them to lie down.

I told Jason, "What that dog did is one of the best things that can happen when you get into this situation. It didn't hurt the cow much but that dog hit so fast and so hard it scared her. The only reason Bob didn't get her by the nose is because she kept it close to the ground so she could stick him with one of her horns and try to kill him." That cow happened to be the main ring leader of the herd and the one that caused all the trouble; but not anymore. She had learned her lesson!

Jason and I were probably 100 feet from the cows and the dogs were half-way between us and them. "Jason, let's walk our horses up a few feet and get the cows moving. If they get out of the walk we'll just send in the dogs."

We started walking our horses toward the cows and they started to head in the right direction. I knew if they got away from us they were going to take off fast so as soon as they got out of the walk I sent Bob and Sport up ahead of them and stopped them. I let the dogs fight them a little bit to ball them up. We rode up closer and called the dogs back. By the time we got to the corrals with the herd we were probably 50 feet from them. They walked right in the corral like they owned it! Jennifer's Dad was going to run over and shut the gate but I told him we were all right. I had laid Sport and Bob down in the gate opening and the cows weren't going anywhere! I got off my horse and walked over to shut the gate.

"I can't believe that was so easy." Jennifer's Dad exclaimed.

"Well, I'm not sure it's all that easy. We don't have them in the trailers yet."

These corrals were not cattle corrals. They were just panels and a bit flimsy at that. I was eager to get the cows away from them and into the trailers. "Let's see if we can get them loaded." I told everyone.

Jennifer's Dad asked, "How are you going to get them loaded?"

"I'll walk in there with my two dogs and load one trailer and then the other one and see if we can't get them all loaded. Jason, you stay outside here so you can help me. If we get in a spot we can get Bob and Sport after them." It didn't take but a few minutes before we got them all in both trailers and shut the gates.

Jennifer's dad was pretty impressed. He kept saying, "I can't believe that was so easy.

"Now I will say it...this one was easy!" I was pretty happy everything went well.

"I can't believe those dogs listen so well." Jennifer exclaimed.

"I use them a lot doing this kind of work. They have to listen. When I give them a command they have to do it...NOW. They can't do it in 30 minutes or 20 steps later."

"Marvin, this was just so nice of you to help us out. It was a real pleasure watching your dogs work." I couldn't help but feel proud about how good my two dogs were!

The biggest problem after we got the cows loaded was I didn't have room for my horses in the trailer. We had a 30 minute run each way to unload the cattle at her place and get back. I told Jennifer what I thought the best way to handle this would be. "We'll put our halters on our horses and loosen up their saddles. We can tie them to these posts and run over to your house, unload the cows, and come back and get the horses. I don't want to take one load of cattle then have you come back to get the rest and find out they've torn down the corrals and run away again!" Jennifer and her Dad agreed and were more than happy to accommodate my plan!

We got the cattle to her house and unloaded them then Jason and I went back and loaded up our horses and dogs. On the way home I told Jason, "People who get me to come out and dog break their cattle never have this kind of problem again. They can hire someone on horseback with only one dog to go out and get their cattle any time."

Ninety percent of the time you can't convince people you can go out with your dogs and round up their cattle in a fraction of the time it usually takes them to do it their way. They just don't believe it can happen. They think they have to go out there and chase their cows on foot or maybe a horse. If I work someone's cows four or five times and I ride up to their property in my truck and trailer, get out with my horse and my dogs, all I have to do is whistle a couple times and those cows will all come into a ball. They know I'm showing up with my dogs and they are going to behave and go where they are told! They won't take off in ten different directions trying to get away! They will get in their pen like the good cows they're supposed to be!

Chapter 32
Whip Went Into the Herd
Summer 2007

I was roping at some friends house one day and they were telling me how much trouble they had getting their roping steers into the corrals at the back of the arena. I told them I would be glad to bring some of my dogs over to work their steers. I knew it wouldn't take my dogs long before they'd have those steers going nicely into the corrals. My friends were more than happy to have me do this.

We ended up making a plan to work the steers the very next day. I let them know I might bring a young dog with me that needed some exposure to this kind of work. This was not a problem either, they wouldn't mind if I brought all my dogs!

The next day I got my trailer hooked up, brushed my horse Badger out really nice then saddled him up. The whole time I'm doing this I'm trying to think about what young dogs and what trained dogs I should take with me. I finally decided to take Hangin' Tree Sport and Cattle Master Chic. That way I could fix whatever any young dog I took messed up.

I decided to take my young dog, Whip since he'd never really seen something as big as what we were going to get ourselves into with my friend's steers.

I had started Whip's training at home with about 8 to 10 calves. Today over at my friends we were going to work about 60 head in a pretty big field and none of those steers were dog broke! Needless to say, it was going to be a pretty good fight for my dogs and a good experience for Whip.

I got the dogs loaded up and told my wife I was leaving. As usual she told me to be careful. Once the goodbyes were out of the way I jumped in my truck and headed out.

When I arrived at the ranch they told me everyone was busy and couldn't lend a hand but a lady there by the name of Sue wanted to know if she could help me. I'm always glad for help so I told her no problem. She got her horse ready then asked what I wanted her to do. I explained to her to just stay with me unless I asked her to ride somewhere else to help. She then asked me what the plan was. I laid it out to her; "Well, we're going to get the dogs out of the truck, ride into the field, attempt to get the cattle all in a big group and hold them together."

Sue looked at me like I was crazy then told me, "Marvin, that's gonna be really hard to do because there's a few steers in the bunch that always want to run off. When they do, all the rest of them steers will just start running everywhere!"

Again I emphasized, "All we have to do is wait for my dogs to get those steers together then we'll move them to the corrals. Trust me, this'll work fine." She seemed pretty excited to see some of those problem steers get their butts kicked!

I got Sport, Chic and Whip out. As soon as we opened the gate to head into the field steers started going everywhere just like she said they would. I told her not to worry; heck, the field was only like 20 acres.

I started riding around the edge of the field and if a steer peeled off from the main group I would tell the dogs to "Get ahead". Those dogs would be instantly at the head of the steer and if he didn't stop he got bit right on the nose. Once a steer got stopped, and especially if he got bit, he would run back to the main herd milling about in the middle of the field.

I just kept riding around the edge of that field by the fence line and my dogs kept stopping everything that tried to run off. It took us about 15 minutes to get them all held up in the middle of the field. At that point I wanted to get the dogs to start moving the herd toward the corrals. As they started to move in mass, some of the steers would charge a dog and the fight would be on. Well Sport and Chic, being more experienced at this cattle business, knew to bite and let go. But poor Whip was so new to this kind of fighting that when one of the steers charged him and he grabbed it by the nose, he wouldn't let go! That steer ran back into the herd with my dog stuck to his nose.

Sue was in a panic when she saw this happen and pretty worried about how poor Whip would fare in the middle of the herd. I just told her he'd be back out in a minute or so. And sure enough, about a minute later, here comes Whip running out of the herd and looking mighty pleased with himself.

We fought with those steers for another 30 minutes or so before we got them all into the corrals. I then suggested to Sue we let them run back out to the field and do it over again. She thought I was nuts but I told her if we did it a few more times those steers would learn to stay together. Then they'd go into the corral a lot easier! So out into the field those steers went!

The second time the whole job of getting those steers back into the corral only took about 20 minutes and the third time it took ten. We ended up stopping after that just to give everybody a break. My dogs were darn happy about all the great work they got to do and I was proud of Whip for doing such a great job on his first trip off the farm.

Chapter 33
Bill's Bucking Bulls
June 2008

I catch cattle for a guy named Bill who happens to raise bucking stock. That means bucking bulls! And any kind of bucking stock means tough, ornery cattle. I've caught cattle for him for years; bulls, cows, calves; whatever he needs.

I got a call from Bill one day when I was out on the road and he sounded frantic. He had about twenty head of one and two year old bucking bulls he'd been keeping in an old chicken barn and they had escaped. He said to me over the phone, "They're down by Newberg in a big ol' field right on the side of Highway 219! And Marvin, there ain't no fences to be seen anywhere!"

The word upset didn't even begin to describe Bill at this point. I know I'd be pretty upset because it was always dangerous gathering bucking bulls, not to mention doing it on a main highway.

He was pretty much pleading with me at this point. "You have to help me Marvin."

"Let me think about what to do and what I'll need then I'll be there." I raced towards home.

I figured my dogs and I could do about anything with cattle and that seems to be the reputation we've acquired but right now I was thinking how that wasn't always a good thing!

Once I was home I started gathering equipment I needed, getting my horse and dogs ready, and hooking up the trailer. I walked to the house to ask my son Jason if he wanted to help. Even though he had plans, he could tell I was really in a bind. He knows I like to do this kind of high stress cattle gathering and so does he so of course he agreed to help. I knew I could count on him.

Jason got his horse Comet ready. I decided to take my Cattle Master Dog, Chic and Hangin' Tree Sport. Once everyone was loaded we drove out to Highway 219 and Bill's bucking bulls!

Jason asked, "What's the plan?"

"Man, I don't even have one," I told him. "This is just not good. We're gonna be right on the side of the highway. There's a lot of traffic there and these bulls are mean. They'll try to fight people, dogs, horses - they don't care!"

We arrived at the spot where the bulls were loose and met Bill and another guy named Kenny.

"Bill, where are we going put them?" I asked right off.

"In this door." And he pointed toward a small building.

"Door?" I guess when he said door, he meant a door about eight feet wide on the side of this chicken barn where he kept them. I was thinking man alive, we had to bring them out of this field and around the corner of these buildings, get them into the end of this barn and through a pretty small opening! I shook my head and wondered how this was going to all play out.

"Well, Jason, let's get our horses and our dogs." We cinched up the saddles, got collars on our dogs and rode to the field.

"What do you think?" Jason asked me.

"Well the first thing is we have to be careful. These bulls will stick a hole in your horse; they don't care. We'll go out in this big field and set up. I'll try to get around them with my horse and dogs and head them this way."

I put Jason, Bill and Kenny each in a different spot around that field then I rode around those bulls. Right away those bulls came at me like they wanted to seriously hurt me and my horse. Sport and Chic were trotting alongside me. My dog Chic happens to be pretty protective of me and my horses so when a bull charged up to us she grabbed him right on the nose! That was the end of that bull. He took off back to the group where he belonged. I hollered at the dogs to get around behind the herd and we started moving them toward the barn.

Kenny had the driveway blocked on foot and Bill was standing there helping to act as a barricade. The bulls came down through the field and around the corner of the barn with me and the dogs following behind them. They all walk single file right back through that eight foot door into the barn. I'm thinking, man, this was just too easy.

Bill shut the door on the barn as I rode up and got off my horse. "Man, I can't even believe that. Those dudes just went right back in." I said to him.

Later I was thinking about the day's event. Bill's cattle were always getting out. If you have cattle and they've been on your property awhile, they always seem to know where it was they got out. That's why a lot of times when you get after them they'll go right back to where they belong using the same path they took to get out! The trick with these bulls was to get them headed the right way and keep them away from the highway. On that day I was sure glad there weren't any accidents and Bill's bulls were back safely on his property ...until the next time!

Chapter 34
My Trip to Las Vegas
June 2008

A friend of mine, Cody, lives in Arizona. He buys dogs from me once in a while. One day he and I were talking on the phone when he asked me, "Hey, did you know I go up north of Las Vegas and catch wild cows once in a while?"

I was thinking that sounded like a lot of fun so I told him, "I sure would like to go."

"Hey if you'd like to go I'll set it up."

"Oh heck yeah! But…" I added, "It's just a long way for me to drive a trailer over with a horse and my dogs."

"Well how about this; I'll just pick you up at the airport in Las Vegas. You don't have to bring anything. I'll bring it all and we'll just take off."

"You have extra horses?"

"You bet," he says, "I have dogs, horses, everything. Just fly into Vegas, get a cab, cruise out to the end of the strip and I'll pick you up." I'm assuming by "strip" he meant the end of the main road through Las Vegas.

I'd never really met this guy in person. I'd only talked to him on the phone when he bought dogs from me. But I sure was ready to go on this adventure!

We set up a time that worked for both of us and I booked a flight. My wife Jodi had a good laugh at me. I guess she just thought I was half crazy for wanting to go gather some wild cows in Las Vegas! She said, "You be careful" as I headed out the door, on my way to the airport and adventure!

When I landed in Las Vegas, I got a cab and cruised to the end of the strip just like we planned. At the end of the "strip" there was a truck stop where I met up with Cody.

He wasn't lying. He had a trailer load of horses and a truck load of dogs. We took off, talking the whole way. It was June and I'd forgotten how hot it gets in Nevada. After a bit of driving we got to a camping spot up in the mountains. The thermometer in the truck said 111 degrees and it was only 1 o'clock in the afternoon! I was thinking, 'Dear God, *what have I gotten myself into?*' but said to Cody, "Man, this is going be rough."

"Oh yeah, I probably should of mentioned it was going to be hot. I haven't been up here in the summer like this. I usually go in the fall or the winter…or the spring." Now he tells me….

Our plan was to stay up in the mountains for a couple days and sleep in the dirt. We actually needed to ride the horses to the spot where Cody wanted us to camp as we couldn't get the truck and trailer up there. We unloaded our gear from the truck and packed it on the horses. The dogs were more than ready to move on out. We cinched up our saddles and rode out.

After a few hours of riding I asked Cody, "How far is it 'til we get to the camp site?"

"About eight miles" he said.

"Well, I guess that ain't too far."

"There's a creek that runs all the way down through this canyon. We'll stop there to cool off."

Well, we found the creek all right but there wasn't any water in it! Thank goodness we had a case of water in our pack saddles. The dogs were hot, we were hot, but we just kept riding. We were riding through bluffs and canyons; places where it was barely wide enough for a horse to get through. After awhile I said, "Dog gone Cody, when is the water gonna show up?"

"I don't know. I don't know how far we have to go before we see some."

"Well, the way I see it is we're darn near out of water by now and we need drinking water if we're spending a night or two up here."

He pointed ahead and said, "If you want to ride ahead, take these water bottles and just follow this dry creek bed up the canyon for a mile or so. That creek has to be running somewhere up there."

Cody handed me the water bottles and I took off on my horse to find some water. I got about two or three hundred yards ahead when I found a little bit in some watering holes. I filled up the bottles and rode back to where Cody and the dogs were waiting.

The dogs were so hot they kept searching for shade. Every time they found a bluff they'd crawl under it trying to cool down and stay out of the sun.

"Man, we have to try and keep those dogs out from under that shade. That's where the rattlesnakes are laying!" Cody called the dogs to him.

I was thinking *'Oh great!'*

We watered the dogs then poured some water on them to cool them off. We continued to ride until we got to this spot where Cody wanted to set up camp. There was an old corral there and some old hay equipment.

I was looking around when it suddenly dawned on me. "My Gosh! People actually lived up here!"

"Oh, yeah," Cody told me, "At one time they did. When they left they just left all their old horse drawn hay equipment."

As we were putting the horses in the corrals I asked Cody, "What are you thinking...like the plan?"

"There's a nice stream heading up from the corral. Let's go up there and see if we can find any cattle before we bed down for the night."

So we just put the pack horses in the corral and kept the riding horses out. We called the dogs then rode out. We rode for a couple hours and all we saw was some old cow pies. No cows, no fresh tracks, no anything.

Cody said, "Wow, they must be way back up in the mountains!"

"And we're not?!" I was a little surprised.

"Oh, no!"

Suddenly I started looking around. There was nothing but mountains surrounding us. I got to thinking *'Gosh dang, this is gonna be a long couple of days!'*

After awhile with no cow sightings, we decided to ride back to camp. It was too hot to build a fire so we ate some cold chili out of the can.

"Man, this is just rough Cody."

He agreed. A little later when the temperature dropped, we went riding around some more. The horse I was on started blowing and snorting and moving sideways until I wasn't sure how I was staying on him but somehow I did.

"Cody, what's wrong with this horse?"

"Aw," Cody said, "a rattle snake probably spooked him!"

After this excitement we headed back to camp and called it a night. Once the horses and dogs were settled we threw down some tarps and rolled out our sleeping bags. We were lying there for a bit before I finally said, "You know what Cody? I'm thinking, let's just saddle up in the morning and pack ourselves on out of here, head back to Las Vegas, and I'll go home."

"You know, I was hoping you'd say that. I think this would be a good trip for the winter time."

"I totally agree."

We tried to sleep but it seemed like every five minutes one of the dogs was growling, or barking, or whining at something. I don't think I got a solid half hour of sleep. Around 4:30 in the morning we finally decided to just get up, saddle up, and head out of there.

Needless to say, it didn't take us nearly as long to get off that mountain in the morning when it was only 80 degrees as it took us to climb it in the afternoon in 111 degrees!

As we were riding down the mountain I asked Cody, "Have you been able to catch cattle out of here before?"

"Oh sure. We bay them up with the dogs and rope them. We dally them up close to our horses and usually with two or three guys we can lead them out of here."

"Well, I sure would like to come back and do it sometime." I really meant it, just not during the summer.

We made it to the truck, packed our stuff up and watered the dogs at the creek.

"Cody, just make sure you keep in touch with me and let me know when you want to try again." I added, "I think we ought to rent a helicopter and have somebody fly us over those mountains when we go back."

"That sounds like a good idea," he chuckled.

I got back to the airport and into a hotel room since I had to change my flight. I couldn't get another one out until the next day. That air conditioning sure felt good!

When I got home I told my wife all about the trip.

"You know Jodi?" I said to my wife, "That's sure not a trip for the middle of summer."

She just shook her head and laughed.

Chapter 35
The Ghost Bull
Summer 2008

Years ago, not long after I met Bill, he called wanting me to catch some of his bucking stock for him. I had my dogs and I usually had anywhere from one to four people I could rely on to help me, depending on who I could get a hold of first.

Bill's cattle were out on 400 acres just outside of Newberg. They were really good about staying in the perimeter fences and on the property but there were a lot of internal cross-fences on the property and they would tear them down like they weren't even there. It wouldn't even slow them down. The cows would go through the fences first and the calves would follow.

The majority of the time the bulls were in their own field or in the corrals so I didn't have to fight many of them. I just had to fight mama cows and their calves or an occasional herd bull.

On this one particular day we were having a heck of a time gathering up the cattle. Bill had one bull that probably weighed 1200 pounds. He was a big, ornery white bull. He would keep the herd out and he was always able to elude us. One minute he would be there and the next minute he would be gone! He was like a ghost!

My wife Jodi was helping that day as well as three or four other people. We had already spent a good part of the day gathering cattle. We had thirty head in the corrals but there should have been about sixty. So we rode out and started looking for the rest of the herd.

We rode out toward the back end of the property which took us across a creek and up a hill. All along the way there were old pieces of broken fence lying in the fields or in the trails where the cattle busted through. Most of the time there was only one strand lying on the ground and it was just enough to trip my horse, Badger. I would get my Leatherman's tool out, cut it out and put it up in the weeds so it could be seen.

We were going along when Badger stepped on a piece of wire. It went between his hoof and his horse shoe. I swung down from the saddle while he stood perfectly still. I was able to cut it out without incident but it was just another one of those hazards to slow us up. I was getting aggravated by then because we had been there for hours and hours that day following these cows. There were many places on the property we couldn't reach because of dense brush or blackberries. It was hot and we were tired. We sent the dogs out to look for the cows but they didn't have any luck. We had about thirty head left to catch and we couldn't even find them they were brushed up so bad.

I told Bill, "Man, that's it. I'm out of here. My horses are tired, my dogs are worn out, and I'm worn out. We're gonna head for the house."

"Man...I really need those other thirty head."

"Well we tried to find them and can't. If you find them see if you can run them down the hill at least then give me a call. We can figure out what to do from there." I knew Bill was disappointed that we were giving up but we were just too worn out to work anymore.

Everyone loaded up their horses, I put the dogs in the back of my truck, and we all left.

The next afternoon I got a call from Bill. He informed me, "We found them but we can't do anything with them. I've got people here on foot; everybody is running around but we just can't get them in the corrals. They are back up in the corner. I know exactly where they are."

"Well...both Jodi and Jason aren't home. I don't have any help but let me see what I can do. Just don't run them out until I call you back."

I got ahold of Jodi on her cell phone and explained the situation. I told her I would saddle up her horse, Tater and head to Bill's and she could meet me there. I was also planning on taking my other horse, Squirt, for Bill's boy to ride. Jodi rearranged her day so she could meet me out at Bill's property to help. Bill was her friend too and she knew he needed to catch these cows.

I got Tyson, Sport and Chic ready and the horses saddled up and loaded. I called Bill to let him know I was on my way. I told him I was bringing a horse for Billy to ride.

I hauled horses and dogs out there and Jodi met me. We pulled the horses from the trailer, cinched up the saddles, let the dogs out and asked Bill where the cattle were. "They're back up there in the corner of the property." I had been on this property before but I had no idea they could get back that far.

We rode to where Bill said they were. I didn't want to get my horse all the way in the corner because it was so overgrown with brush and brambles that I wouldn't have a chance to keep up with the cattle when they came out. I knew they weren't going to walk out of there!

I positioned Jodi and Billy in the spots I thought best for them to be when the cows came out. I rode toward that corner and sent the dogs in to bring the cattle out. I heard the dogs fighting with them when suddenly the cattle came thundering out; they were just a blur going through all the brush! I hollered at Jodi and Billy, "The cattle are coming out."

I loped Badger alongside the cows and kept them headed down an old road and across the field. I knew when we hit the big field we called Table Top the cows would scatter.

Jodi and Billy headed towards the cattle as I was coming along beside them. We got them out in the field and kept them from going down in the brush. They continued to go down the old road. The dogs were running and fighting with them enough to keep them slowed down. I was riding at a pretty good clip with Badger by then. The cows were running straight down that gravel road right to the corrals! They went inside and Bill shut the gate. I couldn't believe it!

I think the day before they fought my dogs so much that when they heard the dogs this time they didn't want anything more to do with them. That big white ghost bull figured he'd lost the battle once we found his hiding spot so he just took all those cows straight to the corrals!

It took us another half an hour to sort out the cattle that needed loading into trailers. Afterwards, we let the dogs and horses cool off then loaded them up in the trucks and headed home.

Chapter 36
Catching Cattle in the Snow
Winter 2009

I was at home one winter day when a man by the name of Stan called. The first thing he said when I answered the phone was "Marvin, I heard you haul cattle."

I told him I'd haul whatever he had so he proceeded to tell me how he bought a small heard of Scottish Highlander cattle that needed hauling back to his property. Of course the first thing that went through my mind is why would someone buy those kinds of cattle but I bit my tongue! I asked Stan where they were located and he told me McMinnville, Oregon in the hills. He also assured me they were really easy to load - just back the trailer up to the fence and they'd practically load themselves. Generally I always have a positive outlook and a lot of confidence, but when it comes to Scottish Highlander Cattle and the words "easy-to-load" I wasn't too sure those went together. Stan and I talked a bit more and came up with a plan to haul them the following Saturday.

Saturday morning came around and I was getting ready to pick Stan up at his house around nine before driving out to the cattle. Unfortunately I'd been awake since four that morning thinking about these cows. I just had this sinking feeling it was probably not going to be all that easy. The weather man on early morning TV was predicting snow in the mountains; right where we were headed to pick up these cattle.

I started getting my stuff ready for this "easy" cattle gathering event. I loaded my dog boxes on the back of my truck so my dogs had a dry place to wait if the weather turned really nasty. I hooked up my goose neck trailer because it was a little bigger then my old bumper pull I normally used for hauling cattle. By the time I was hooked up and had my dogs Sport and Chic loaded, I still had a couple of hours to kill so I drove into town for some breakfast before picking up Stan.

When I arrived at Stan's place he showed me where he wanted those Highlander cattle unloaded. One quick look around his property and I told him he sure had a lot of nice fence to be owning these type of cattle! He assured me again that the people who sold them told him they were easy keepers. Once again I really had to bite my tongue.

As we drove out of McMinnville and started into the hills it began to snow. I emphasized to Stan how important it was that these cows load quickly into the trailer so we could get out of the hills before we got stuck in the snow!

When we reached the property where the cattle were the man who sold them to Stan was there with his family. He told us the cattle would go right into the trailer if everyone just stood back and he went into the trailer with some grain. It was a tight area I had to back into so it took me awhile to get the trailer situated. Once I parked it I opened up the back gate, got out of the way and hoped the loading went fast as snow dusted my hat. The guy who owned the cattle started working his magic and one old cow jumped right into the trailer…then a calf went in. And that was where the loading stopped. None of the others would go in. The guy told his wife and son to get behind the cows and help "shoo" them into the trailer.

By now it was snowing hard and I was thinking how I had to back down a hill to park in this spot. I was sure hoping we'd get out of there soon so I'd make it back up the hill in the snow with a load of cattle!

The whole family was helping by this time and it was only getting worse. The cows that were in the trailer came back out and now nothing would go in. The guy asked me and Stan to help shoo the cows into the trailer. After about 10 minutes of running around with cows going every which way but in the trailer I quit and stepped aside to watch. A bit more time passed with no cows loading in the trailer when I finally told Stan we either had to get the cattle in the trailer or leave them because I needed to get out of there before I was stuck in the snow. Everyone was cold, wet and tired of chasing cows. Stan asked me what I'd do.

"How about if I get my dogs out, have everyone stay out of the way, and I'll put them to work on these cows?"

Both Stan and the guy who sold him the cattle were more than happy at this point to let someone else take over. I walked to the truck and unload the dogs. As soon as the dogs got in the field one of the cows decided to charge Chic. Chic didn't run from anything. So when my little 32 pound dog locked her sharp teeth into the head and nose of that 1000 pound cow, she quickly decided she loved my trailer and jumped right in! One of the little calves tried to leave the scene. She ran off a little ways and jumped a low fence that looked like it'd been jumped many times in the past. The guy who owned the cattle was hollering at me wanting to know what I was going to do now. Heck, that was no big deal since that little calf stopped once it got on the other side of the fence. I told Sport to "Go get 'em". He ziped under the fence and got around that calf. The fight was on between that calf and Sport but after about thirty seconds the little calf wanted mommy so bad she jumped back over the fence!

We'd gotten two of the main problem cows whipped at this point so it only took about two more minutes and the dogs had all the cattle in the trailer.

Once the cattle were loaded and the door was shut and latched, the guy asked me why I didn't use my dogs in the beginning. I told him that every time I get my dogs out to work cattle I take a chance of getting them hurt or killed and since he had told me they would easily load with grain I figured I'd give the dogs a break. Obviously that didn't happen but luckily for my dogs all went well!

Once the dogs were in their boxes Stan and I made our exit and just in time too as we barely got the truck out of the loading spot.

On the way back to Stan's property we talked about cow dogs and loading cattle. I told Stan my favorite hobby is catching cows with dogs.

When we arrived at Stan's property we unloaded the cattle. I told him not to forget I haul cattle whether I have to catch them or not!

A few months later Stan called me and asked if I would haul his herd off his property. He sold all of them because they were too hard on his fences! I hauled them to the new owner's property a few days later. The best part was when I went to pick them up from Stan's property it didn't take but a few quick minutes for Chic and Sport to load the whole lot of them!

Chapter 37
My Two Missing Calves
Winter 2009

It was one cold winter. A friend and I had some cattle we were partners on that we kept on his property. He happened to be on vacation, probably somewhere warm, while I was home taking care of the cattle. His property wasn't too far from my place so it really wasn't any problem for me to do this. I had been going over to his place to feed the cattle for a few weeks and everything was going great; no problems at all. Then on this one day when I was heading up the lane to his barn I saw a couple of calves out and the first thing I thought was how I didn't want these calves coming down the lane and getting on the road or in his yard. So I closed the gate that led into the lane and went back to my house a couple of miles away to get a dog. I decided I didn't need a horse because these calves knew where they got out and I was sure they'd go right back through the fence where they got out without a chase or the need to rope them.

I decided to take my dog Tyson. I loaded him into my truck, put his collar on, then drove back to put those two calves in the field where they belonged. I pulled up to the gate and opened it, drove in and shut it behind me in case the calves got by me and Tyson. I drove as close to where those calves were as I could. I unloaded Tyson and once he was off that truck he was all business. He knew something fun was about to happen and to Tyson, fun was working cows.

The way I saw it, the calves could go left and run back through the fence or they could go right but Tyson would have to stop them because I didn't want them going that direction. I sent Tyson a little to the right to try to keep them from going that way as I walked up to them. One calf ran back through the fence so fast I started thinking this was going to be easy work! Right as I was having that thought the other calf charged me. I jumped to the side and Tyson ran to get ahead of this angry calf and keep him off of me. Once Tyson got in front of him he stopped and just stood there. I told Tyson to lie down and hold him there. It seemed like it was going to be a fight to get that calf to go through the fence so I walked up to the corner where these calves had been milling about and opened the gate up there. I wanted to just run those calves back through the fence but now that Tyson had this calf stopped I figured it'd be easier if we just moved him through the gate rather than get in a big fight with him. I just had to make sure the rest of the herd didn't try to get out of the open gate.

Once I was out of the way I told Tyson to walk up to the calf. As Tyson moved in closer to the calf, he started walking to the corner where the open gate was. He kept looking at the cows on the other side of the fence but wouldn't go through the fence like the other calf did so I had Tyson keep him walking up the fence line. Once the calf saw the open gate he went through it. I closed the gate, petted Tyson and told him what a good job he'd done. After making sure the gates were secure I got the tractor out, loaded hay, feed all the cows and checked to make sure the water tanks were full. When I finished I put the tractor back in the barn where it belonged, had Tyson load up on the truck, and drove home.

The next morning I was out feeding my calves at home when I got to counting them and saw I was missing a couple of black calves. So I counted them again and sure enough I had two black calves missing. That got me thinking how I had just run two loose black calves back into my friend's field. So later that day when I went back to feed the cows at his place, I noticed that sure enough, there were two black calves that weren't mixing with the rest of the herd. They were my two missing calves!

Later that day I was telling my wife how I found my two calves. She thought it was pretty darn funny that I didn't even know they were gone until after I caught them!

Chapter 38
Those Are Our Steers Over There
Spring of 2009

I was at a roping practice one evening when my friend Wiley asked if I was busy the next morning. I asked what he had in mind and he told me he and some other folks were going to gather about forty head of roping steers. Unfortunately the steers were in a field that wasn't very user-friendly. The corrals had to be put at the side of the field instead of the corner due to the amount of mud from the wet Oregon spring. He told me they had a nice corral in one of the corners but they couldn't get to it because of the mud. He said he'd really like to have somebody along who knew cows and had some good cow dogs! I told him I'd meet him out there the next morning.

I got up early to get everything ready. I fed my horse first thing so he could have some time to enjoy his breakfast before I saddled him then I let my dogs out so they could run and play for awhile before being loaded. I decided to do all the chores while my horse was eating and my dogs were playing. About that time my employees showed up so I talked to them about the day's fence job and made sure they had everything they needed to get started. Once those guys were on their way I set about to loading everything I'd need for the day.

I was thinking that before we even got to the steers it was going to be rough on my dogs because of where the corrals were located and how much mud they'd have to work in. I was trying to decide what dogs I wanted to take while I brushed and saddled Badger. I loaded Badger in the trailer then got my ropes - you never know when you might have to rope a steer or two. I threw those in my rope bag then went to get the dogs. I decide to take four with me. I took my faithful Hangin' Tree Sport and Cattle Master Chic. I also chose Tyson who is a son of Sport and Chic. He was new to this 'out-in-the-field' kind of cattle work. I decided to get even crazier and bring along Hangin' Tree Trap. I was thinking I might just be a bit nuts taking along Trap and Tyson. Those two are on their way to being great working dogs but they were still young and inexperienced so it could make for a long day! But I figured Sport and Chic would keep me out of trouble with Tyson and Trap. This was a great opportunity to put some good cattle experience and training on them.

After loading the dogs I stopped at the house on my way out to say goodbye to my wife Jodi. As usual, she told me to be careful.

I drove to the ranch to meet up with everyone. I was thinking this just might end up being a lot of fun. When I arrived at the ranch we all got to do our 'meet-and-greet' before heading out to where the herd was located. I followed my buddy, Wiley, because I had no idea where we were going. The drive took about 30 minutes. Once we were all parked I got out and asked Wiley what needed to be done. He explained to me that the cattle were back in the far corner of the woods and we just needed to get them in the corral which was close to where we'd all parked. Since I had the only horse, everyone was planning on hanging back and watching while I went out to gather the cattle! I got Badger out of the trailer, tightened his cinch and put the bridle on him. Then I unloaded the dogs from my truck and I had to be extra careful since we were only about 20 feet from a really busy highway.

Once I got the collars on the dogs and made my way across the field I could see some of the cattle tucked way back in the woods. I was heading toward them and the dogs were ready to go to work now that they could see the cattle. I knew it was going to be a little tough to work four dogs like this, especially once I got back by the corrals. Mainly this was because Tyson and Trap weren't all that well trained yet. But they had to learn some day so it might as well be today. I knew at least Sport and Chic would listen to me!

When I reached the edge of the woods there was an open gate I had to bring the cattle back through so I had Sport lay to the right side of the gate. This was so he could help me guide the cattle into the big field when they come through and we could keep them from turning around and tearing back through the fences into the woods. I entered the woods through the gate and went to my right thinking that was the easiest way to get around the cattle. There was a bad corner in that direction and I wanted to keep the cattle away from it. All my dogs were working together really well at the moment, almost as if they knew this wasn't a good place to start fighting cows. I sent Chic and Tyson around to the back side of the cattle and kept Trap with me in case the cattle tried to get by the gate on my side.

It took the dogs, all working together, about 5 minutes to get the herd through the gate. When the last steer passed through, I sent the dogs to "Get ahead" and stop the herd. Once the cattle were stopped it should be an easy job for the dogs to keep them in the field. I had the dogs fan out around the herd then made them all lie down so the cattle could settle.

After a few minutes of rest, the dogs and I moved the cattle across the field to the corrals. Several times some of those steers tried to get away but I had way more dog-power than they wanted to mess with so it was pretty easy to keep the herd together.

This whole procedure took about 20 minutes and ended when we had them in the corral and I shut the gate. I got off my horse and loosened the cinch then reached down to pet my dogs for a job well done. Right about that time I heard Mike, a guy from the group, yell out that he thought there were some of our steers on the other side of the pasture fence. I always looked forward to a situation like this because it was usually where the challenges came into play and where I could really test how well my dogs handled tough situations! I wanted to take a look at what I was up against so I bridled Badger back up and tightened his cinch.

I knew that if the cattle were on the wrong side of the fence it might be tough getting them back on the right side. I took Sport and Chic with me but left Tyson and Trap in their kennels this time. The two dogs and I head over to where Mike said he saw the steers. It was only a few hundred yards to the fence. Mike met me there on foot and sure enough, we saw two steers on the wrong side! The big problem was we weren't seeing a way to get them back. Good thing I had my Leatherman tool on me. Mike didn't want to cut the barbed wire or the woven wire so I ended up taking off the wire clips that held the wire to the metal posts. Then Mike stretched the barbed wire to the top of the t- posts. He pushed the woven wire down some with his boot, at least enough that the steers could jump over it. I told Mike that all I needed to do was lift Sport and Chic over the fence and they'd go back in the brush and convince those steers to jump back through the fence. It sure sounded easy coming out of my mouth. Maybe it was a good thing that my dogs couldn't talk. There were times when I believed they could do just about anything. But if they could talk I bet they would tell me to go ahead and gather up the steers myself while they watched!

I set both Sport and Chic over the fence and told them to hunt up those steers. It only took a minute or so before they had both those steers back at the fence. But the steers were having nothing to do with jumping through the wire. So I did some quick thinking and decided to position Chic at an angle to the opening I wanted the steers to jump through then I had Sport bring them on a path toward Chick. As they were coming toward the fence and saw Chic in front of them they stopped. At that moment I gave the command for Sport to bite them. Sport shot in really fast and bit the closest one to him. Afraid to go towards Chic but needing to go somewhere, it jumped through the opening in the fence with the other one following right behind. After I lifted my dogs back on the other side of the fence we put the wire back in place as best we could. Mike told me he'd come back to fix the fence later.

I headed for the corrals and the dogs brought in those last two steers behind me. When I mentioned how I thought everything went smoothly, there was no one who disagreed with me!

I put up my horse and dogs then stayed to help load the cattle. When that was finally done I headed home and back to my regular day job of building fence.

Chapter 39
One Wild Calf
August 2009

One day when I got home from work and checked my email there was a message from a guy who lived near Albany, Oregon. He wanted to know if I had a dog for hire. When I called back to ask what was going on, he told me he'd bought a calf and it ran away when he was trying to load it in his trailer. She had run through six fences already and the next one would land her in a subdivision! At the moment she was in a field with about eight lamas!

I told him I would come and catch her but it would take me a bit to get there because he was about 100 miles south of me.

I asked my son, Jason, if he wanted to go. He loved the wild situations I got into so he was more than happy to help! I also called a buddy of mine, Tim, from Cottage Grove and asked if he wanted to meet up with us. He was just as excited to join the fun as Jason.

Jason and I loaded up my horse Badger and his horse Comet. Then we loaded up the real help; Hangin' Tree Sport and his side-kick, Chic, a female Cattle Master dog. Once we were loaded we headed down to Albany where we met with the guy who owned the calf.

The guy asked me what I had in mind. I explained to him that I would try and get the dogs to hold up the calf and Jason and I would rope it.

We saddled up and rode over to where the calf was and sure enough there were a lot of llamas around. Fortunately the people who owned them had them all haltered and tied up.

Well, the horses didn't care much for the llamas but we got past them and into the field where the calf was. The guy was right. One more fence and that calf would have been in the neighboring subdivision! Somehow I don't think those people would have appreciated that!

We all discussed what to do and came up with a plan. It only took us about five minutes to get the calf stopped and bayed-up with the dogs! Hangin' Tree Cowdogs make gathering cattle an easy job.

Once the dogs got their part of the job done I was able to get a rope on the calf and Jason roped her back feet. Then he and Tim tied her down and together we slid her into the trailer. We tied the calf and loaded her this way because the guy had a small, open-top single axle trailer and we weren't sure that calf wouldn't jump out.

The main reason the situation went bad for this guy was because he didn't get the calves loaded correctly. He bought two calves and when he went to load them in the trailer one went in and one went by the outside of the trailer. The one that didn't make it in the trailer went wild and crazy because it couldn't find its partner. That's what happens when cows who are used to being together get separated. When they tried to stop her she got more crazed and started bashing through fences. That's when he decided to call us!

One of the luckiest things that happened that day, besides how easy our dogs made the job, was a lady who stopped and took a lot of pictures. She was kind enough to load them on a disc and mail them to us.

It's always fun to go back through pictures and see how it looked from an observer's point of view!

Chapter 40
My Calves Are On the Highway
Summer 2009

One day I was out building fence, not because I especially enjoy building fence but because I own Marvin's Fencing and that's what I do for a living. I was right in the middle of putting up some wire strands when my neighbor, Dave, called my cell and hollered, "Marvin, your cows are up on the road loose by your house."

This was not a good situation so I jumped in my truck and took off for home. I stopped by Dave's house and picked him up so he could help me. We were headed back to my house when I saw my three calves. They were on the side of the road about a half mile from my house grazing in a field that was not fenced. If those calves decided to go down into the nearby canyon I might have to spend days trying to find them. This was not a good spot for them to be. Or maybe it was a good spot for them to be but not a good spot for me to have them in!

Dave asked, "What are you going to do?"

"We'll run back to my place so I can grab my little John Deere Gator and a couple dogs, shoot back here real quick then try to push those calves up on this gravel road. If we can get them on the road then my dogs will keep 'em following me on the Gator."

"Really?" Dave seemed a bit skeptical "That easy huh?"

"Well, Yeah…I hope. If we can get them up on this road it will be." I knew my calves. I had worked them with my dogs many times. They respected my dogs and would follow my gator if there was a dog behind them.

We got to the house, swapped my truck for the Gator, took the dogs out of their kennels and started back to where the calves were. We were just heading up the road when here came those calves trucking along the gravel road back towards home! As soon as they saw us though they turned tail and took off the wrong way back up the hill!

"Oh crud!" Dave said, "What are we going to do now?"

"Hang on…I gotta stop and turn these dogs loose." I skid the Gator to a stop and quickly unchained my dogs, Sport and Chic. I give them the command to "Get ahead" and they jumped off the gator and took off after the calves. The dogs overtook the calves a couple hundred feet down the road, got them stopped and headed back towards us.

Dave had never seen my dogs work cattle in a real-life situation. He was amazed!

"Now what happens with them?" he asked.

"Oh I'll just drive along this road and the dogs will make those calves follow us. We just have to make sure we're going fast enough so they don't pass us!"

The dogs brought the calves toward the Gator and I turned it around and headed the other way before they got ahead of me. I went up another neighbor's driveway because that was the shortest way back to the field where I wanted to put them. Sport and Chic brought the cattle along at a nice little trot. They followed me up the gravel driveway toward that neighbor's house. Luckily the neighbor's dogs weren't out in the yard to cause any trouble. We went up the driveway and I put the calves into the pasture.

"That was just too easy. What are you going to do with them now since they're not in your field?"

"That shouldn't be any problem," I said, "I'll just open the other gate and kick them back into my own field. But I guess I first have to run around my fence line and see where they got out."

Getting those calves back into my field was just a matter of opening another gate and having my dogs spend about 2 minutes pushing them through it. What really took the longest time was finding out where they got out and then fixing the fence. Fortunately it gave Sport and Chic a nice opportunity to romp and play in the field while I strung fence! And when that was done I got in my pickup and went back to building fences on my other job!

Chapter 41
Not My Calves
Summer 2009

It seems every time there are loose cattle roaming around the mountain where I live people call me because they think they're mine or think I might know who they belong to.

One day I was out on a fence job when I got a call about two calves running around on the road about a half mile from my house. Based on the description of where they were seen my first thought was they belonged to a neighbor of mine. Since I hate to hear about anyone's cattle being on the road, I let my fence crew know that I'd be gone for a bit and then headed home.

I called my neighbor, Jim, on the way.

"Hey Jim, I just got a call about two calves running loose on Mountain Home road near Bell road. I'm thinking they're probably either yours or mine."

"Oh Shoot! I better run out and count my herd!" Jim said.

He was about ready to hang up when I said, "Well look here, I'm on my way to the house. I'll grab a couple of dogs then head over your way to where those calves were last seen."

"Sounds good, Marvin. I'll call you back!" Jim quickly got off the phone. I could tell he was anxious to check if the calves were from his herd.

I drove by the spot where the calves were supposed to be as I was making my way home but I didn't see them so at least they weren't on the road. When I got to the house I pulled Sport and Chic out of their kennels, get their collars on and loaded them in my truck. I drove to the last spot the calves were seen. Once I got there I unload the dogs and made my way into the woods where I was hoping I'd find the calves. I was thinking that if they were in the woods than between me and the dogs we could get them back through the fence and into Jim's field. Unfortunately Jim didn't have a cell phone so I couldn't call him to coordinate for any assistance on his side of the woods and he hadn't called me back or shown up.

After some tromping around in the woods I wasn't able to find the calves or Jim. So I finally called his house and he answered the phone.

"Hey," I said to him, a bit of irritation in my voice, "I'm over by your fence in the woods and I can't find any calves. Are you gonna come out and help me look for them?"

"Oh…well I counted my herd and they're not my calves so I didn't bother coming out." There's a few moments of silence before he adds, "um…do you need my help?"

"Well, I could sure use it – that's if we can even find these calves."

I kept looking for the calves while waiting for Jim to show up. About 15 minutes later the dogs finally found them and the fight was on. Luckily for me they were still in the woods and blackberries and not on some other road miles away. The dogs got the calves held up in the blackberries about the time Jim showed up. We were finally able to get a good look at the calves. Right away I could tell they weren't my calves either but I could see they were in good shape so we talked it over and decided to put them in Jim's field with his herd until we could find their owner.

In order for our plan to proceed, we needed to take the barbed wire fence down enough so we could get the calves through it and onto Jim's property. We didn't have any fence tools with us and it was a long walk to either my truck or his house. Fortunately I had my handy Leatherman on me so I start pulling staples. We pulled the top two strands of wire loose and stretched them on top of a pair of posts. The third strand we loosened and pushed to the ground where we tied it down. At this point I felt the dogs could bring the calves over and run them through the fence. We moved out of the way and I told Sport and Chic to "Bring 'em". It took a few minutes for the dogs to convince the two calves that they needed to go through the fence but they got it done. Once they were through we fixed the fence.

I had to get back to work so Jim said he'd call the county and let them know the calves were at his house. I drove back to my house to put the dogs up and once I had them taken care of I went back to my fence job. Of course as soon as I got to the job site the guys wanted to take a break and hear all about what happened!

About a week later Jim called me. "Well Marvin, seems like those calves got claimed. Only problem is the owners don't have a way to haul them so they want to hire you to deliver them back to their house."

I told Jim, "Not a problem. Give me an address and I'll see you tomorrow to pick those calves up! By the way, you want to come along?"

"You bet!"

The next day I loaded up my horse Badger and my dogs, Sport and Chic. I called Jim on my way over and we decided we'd bring all the cattle into his corral. It would just make it a lot easier to separate out those two calves.

It was pretty quick work getting them all in the corral with the dogs and horse. Once we got the two calves sorted off we turned the others back out to the field. We loaded the calves into my trailer, locked them in the front part then loaded Badger in the back portion. I put Sport and Chic in the truck. We made sure all the gates were shut and locked before heading to the calf owner's property; no sense in having to gather our own loose cattle when we got back.

When we arrived at the address we were given, the calf owners came out to greet us and their calves. We got to talking and they told us how they raise a couple of calves every year and this is the first time they had gotten out. I think these folks got to feeling pretty comfortable real quick because soon they were telling us how long they had lived on their property and how they had been married 50 years. Eventually we figured we should probably unload the calves! It took me several tries to back into the spot they wanted them unloaded – it was tight and narrow. But, I managed it and got those calves unloaded without incident.

As I was loading up and getting ready to head out, the calf owners asked me if they could hire me to move their calves down the road in a couple of months to a field they had rented. I told them sure and gave them my number then left. After I dropped off Jim I went home, unloaded the horse and dogs, got everything put up then unhooked the trailer.

It was a couple of weeks later when the calf owners called and wanted me to move their calves. I asked them if I needed to bring my dogs.

"Aw no, those calves should follow the grain bucket right into the trailer." The old fellow told me.

I figured since my dogs liked to ride in the truck anyway I'd just bring them along. I also called Jim, told him I was going to go haul those calves again and asked if he wanted to ride along.

I arranged to pick Jim up in an hour. I did the usual prep with my equipment although this time I left my horse, Badger, at home. Last thing I did before heading out was load up Sport and Chic.

Jim and I drove over to get the calves who probably at this point in time weighed about 900 lbs each. When we got there it again took some driving finesse to back up to the gate where I needed to load the calves. We got out of the truck, said our hellos then opened the gate on the corral and my trailer. I left my dogs in the truck figuring *'grain'* was going to do the work for us this time. The owner got his grain bucket and walked into the trailer. He rattled that bucket a few times and soon enough those calves came zipping on over. Well they went right up to the back end of the trailer but they wouldn't step in! The old fellow's wife told him to try something else but no matter what he tried they still wouldn't go in. By this time I climbed the fence into the corral to help shoo them into the trailer but they start getting ornery and tried to run us over. Jim also tried to help but nothing was working

The owners don't know what to do and they were clearly frustrated. The little lady asked me what I would do. Well as usual I told her I would get the dogs out and use them to load the calves. She seemed a little skeptical that my dogs could actually get the calves loaded. Both she and her husband told me how they've never seen dogs work cattle before. I explained that I always use my dogs to work cattle but warned that their calves would probably get bit a little in the beginning. Well of course they wanted to know why the dogs needed to bite the calves. I explained that the calves would probably try and run my dogs off initially and in order to make them respect the dogs and move away from them they needed to get bit a time or two on the nose. Since we'd been trying to load these calves for probably 30 minutes and everyone was hot and tired from all the fighting, the lady told me she didn't mind if her calves got bit some and for me to go ahead and let the dogs try.

I went over to the truck and let Sport and Chic out and that lady almost dropped her jaw in surprise when she saw my little 50 pound dogs. "Are you sure those two little dogs are going to be able to load my two big calves?"

"Well, I sure hope so ma'am!" Of course I was just joking with her but she sure did give me a funny look…like I might be a little crazy.

I'm not a big fan of having people in the corral when I'm working my dogs because the calves might run a person over trying to get away from the dogs. Jim got out of the corral because he knew this but the fellow who owned the calves stayed put. I started working the calves a little but I could see that this guy was going to get hurt if I keep at it so I stopped the dogs and called them to me.

"What's wrong?" the lady hollered over to me.

"Well ma'am, I won't work the dogs when there are people in the corral...just too dangerous." I was appealing to her as her husband seemed dead-set on staying in there to help me!

"Roland! Get out of there!" she yelled at him.

"I'm helping Marvin and the dogs!" He yelled back at her a little indignant.

"You know Roland," I stepped in to say, "It's just too hard for the dogs to work with you in the pen but I tell you what...if we need you back in I'll let you know." He seemed to be okay with this but I felt he might have been a little disappointed he couldn't be in the middle of all the excitement!

Once he left the pen it took Sport and Chic about 5 minutes to get the calves into the trailer! The owners were so excited seeing how the dogs worked that they had to tell me over and over again how they'd never seen such amazing dogs. Good ol' Sport and Chic, always the stars of the show.

After the calves were secured in the trailer I asked the fellow where we were going to take them. He told me he would ride with me if I didn't mind and didn't think it were too dangerous. I think he was kidding!

We drove out a little ways to this field where we were planning on unloading them. The guy who owned the field came out to meet us when we arrived. I asked him where he wanted the calves exactly and as soon as he pointed the field out I told the fellow who owned the calves that there was no way they would stay in that fence. Well the guy who owned the pasture said they would. There was definitely some disagreement here! Finally I told Roland they were his calves and I'd unload them but I really emphasized how they'd probably be out within the next day or so. The property owner bristled at this and started to point out how good his fence was. I tried to explain to them both that it didn't matter to me except I know how hard it'd be to find and catch two calves out in that area. They talked for a few minutes quietly. The property owner finally convinced Roland that his calves would stay put so I backed up and unloaded them. Once they were in that field I was done with them.

When I dropped Roland off at his house I told him to give me a call if he needed them hauled again. On the way back to my place Jim told me he didn't think those calves were going to stay put. I agreed and thought about how hard it would be to find them in all those canyons and brush. After dropping off Jim, I went home, put my dogs up and unhooked my trailer. I was done with those calves!

The next morning Roland called me and said his calves were on the loose again because they'd gotten out of the fence. I said I was sure sorry to hear that. I was nice enough to not mention my very prediction of this event the day before! Since I just hate hearing that anyone has livestock loose I told him to give me a call if they spotted those calves and I would help catch them. I think it was about 3 weeks before they found them. Somehow they managed to get them into a nearby corral and loaded in some guy's trailer—then promptly took them to the sale barn.

Chapter 42
What Do Your Dogs Do
When You're Not Home
February 2010

I believe stock dogs are not meant for everyone. In my line of work gathering cattle I see a lot of dogs and I also see a lot of people who can't make their dogs behave and don't really know how to train them properly. If you don't have a well-behaved and well-trained stock dog they will tend to work stock when they feel like it and it may not be according to your plan. It often doesn't matter whether it's a cow, horse, goat, or chickens, they will work it; and I've seen this happen more times than I care to count!

One day I was building a fence for some clients. The people owned a blue heeler and it was allowed to run loose. I was there early in the morning before the owners left for work. As soon as they were gone their dog started chasing and biting at their horses in the corral. I was there the whole day and their dog continued to harass the horses. He would chase them, wait for a while then start in again.

As soon as the dog heard the owners truck coming down the drive at the end of the day he ran out to the driveway and laid down waiting to greet them. They got out of the truck and the dog ran over to get his usual pat on the head, acting like the sweet and well-behaved dog they thought he was!

The man came over to me and we started talking.

"Do you know your dog had been chasing and biting at your horses most of the day?" I asked him

"No way, my dog would never do that!" He sputtered, somewhat indignant.

"Well, you might want to sneak home some day and see what your dog does while you're gone!" I said, just offering some friendly advice. Hopefully he does that someday and then takes the necessary steps to make sure his dog or his horses don't get hurt.

Often times when I'm out building fences I see dogs that chase horses and cattle when they're not supposed to. And too many times owners just laugh. They don't understand what kind of damage their dogs can cause. If the truth were known, I bet horses and livestock suffer needless hurt due to unruly, untrained dogs.

Of course no owner wants to part with their dog even if they are unruly. This means that owners are almost forced to figure out how to keep their dogs out of trouble if they want to keep them around horses and livestock.

My solution in these situations, or for any working dog, is to keep them in nice kennels with good runs. Let them out to run and play at least every morning and evening under SUPERVISION, even if they have a large turnout that's well fenced.

I work my dogs on cattle regularly and start basic obedience with them when they're just pups. Between the cattle training, the constant obedience work, nice kennel setups, and good supervision, I know my dogs won't be wreaking havoc with my livestock or anyone else's, whether I'm home or not!

Chapter 43
Loading Two Bulls
Winter 2010

One day my buddy Kenny called me. He said, "Man, my neighbor cut my fence and my bulls are over in one of his pastures. I don't have a way to load them and get them out."

I knew this was not a good situation because he had two big-horned black bucking bulls and these were not the easiest cattle to work with!

"Do you want to bring some dogs over and help me?" He asked.

"Sure," I told him. "I'll be right over."

"Hey Marvin," he said before hanging up, "One of them bulls is the one we dog broke a while back." I was glad to hear that because it meant the job of catching them might just go a little easier and safer.

I loaded up my dogs Trap, Tyson, and Dottie. My dog Tyson is the son of Sport and Chic and he is one tough dog so I felt I was well-armed for this bull gathering expedition!

I got to Kenny's place and looked the situation over. In order to make a plan I had to know what I was dealing with. The neighbor's pasture was about five acres; the fence was woven wire with a strand of hot wire across the top; and we needed a trailer to load the bulls into.

"I think I'll just back my trailer up to that gate over there, put up a couple panels and we can put them in that way." Kenny said.

"Sounds good to me" I agreed. I decided to use Tyson to begin with because I had good control with him. We set up the trailer with two panels and an old piece of gate coming off of it to form a make-shift loading chute. Then we went on foot into the pasture.

Kenny told me as we approached the bulls, "You need to watch that one bull. He'll charge you."

"No kidding?" I was glad I had Tyson with me.

"The only thing you have going for you," Kenny said, smiling, "is supposedly they'll charge a smaller person first!"

"Well, I guess that is good because you're a lot smaller then me!"

"Yeah, they'll charge the smaller person but they'll fight the one they can catch! I think I might be faster than you Marvin!" Kenny starts laughing at this. Again, I'm just glad I have Tyson with me. Maybe I'll have to sic him on Kenny if that bull comes after us, just so I can get away. Now that got me laughing!

When we were a short distance away from the bulls I sent Tyson out ahead to "Get 'em" and pretty soon he was fighting with these bulls and driving them toward the trailer but it didn't look like we were going to have much luck loading them. We could get them down by the trailer but as soon as we did they keep turning and running back through us. I ran over to the truck and untied Trap so both he and Tyson could work together. Kenny reminded me again how the one bull would charge.

"Well, they're not gonna like my dogs!" I started laughing, "In fact, I think I'll just get Dottie out and carry her around. That way they won't charge me at all!"

The dogs, Kenny and I started working and fighting these bulls and it was taking a long time. We finally got those bulls right up to the trailer, where all they had to do was take one step up, when they'd turn and charge back through us! They charged through Kenny, me, and the dogs like we weren't even there!

This went on for a while; we would get them close to the trailer then they would turn back and run or charge! One of the bulls took off after Kenny. I had to sic Tyson on him as a distraction so Kenny could get away.

Finally the one bull I had dog-broke six months earlier jumped into the trailer and we shut the gate.

Now we just had the other bull to deal with. Kenny and I were talking and trying to decide what to do. I knew we had to be careful. If this bull got mad enough he was just going take off and "leave the country"! We decided the best thing to do was keep working with the dogs on that bull and wear him out some.

The bull turned and ran into an old barn that was nearby and it took us awhile to get him out. Then he tore down a piece of hot wire fence and was running around dragging it all over the place. That made it especially dangerous for us and the dogs. In the middle of all this excitement I hollered over to Kenny, "We have to keep the pressure on him. Any where he goes the dogs need to be right there." We kept moving the bull around and anytime he tried to run off I sent the dogs to stop or turn him. He was pawing and snorting with his nostril flaring but we finally got him over to the panels we had set up. We closed them together so he was trapped in a small pen right in front of the trailer.

This bull was fighting mean mad. He was trying to hook us with his horns, butt us and do anything he could to make us go away. Fortunately he didn't want to go near the dogs at this point. As long as I keep them on the outside of the panels the bull wasn't trying very hard to break out of the pen. It was a little dicey but we managed to get the trailer gate open. The first bull, the one inside, was not coming out; he'd had enough of the dogs. The bull in the pen was mad and circling around in it, and in all honesty he could have torn it down anytime he wanted if it weren't for the dogs patrolling the outer perimeter. And even then if he got mad enough he could easily tear a panel down, run them over, and get away! Kenny suggested, "Let's just wait and see what he does." We backed off a little and I made the dogs lie down around the pen. After a few moments the bull settled down and calmly walked to the trailer, looked at us, and jumped inside like that was his intention all along! Boy, did we shut that door in a hurry! Another fine example of how a job gets done by the work of two cow dogs and two cowboys in one big field with lots of bull!

Chapter 44
Sport's Last Cattle Drive
Spring 2010

One nice spring day I was at the house loading up dogs and horses for a cattle gathering in Othello Washington. I couldn't decide whether to take Sport or leave him at home because of his age and health. I wasn't sure if he'd be able to keep up with the other dogs. In the end I decided to take him. I figured I'd just pick and choose when I'd use him to help gather cattle.

Once loaded and my goodbyes said to my family, I drove to Othello, Washington with my horse and dogs. It was a long drive but once I arrived we got right to work. Sometimes it gets a little boring gathering cattle and moving cows so I asked these folks I was helping if they had anything for me to do that might be a bit more challenging. They told me that the neighbors down the way had some cows they couldn't catch. Some of them had been running loose for over three years! I told my buddy David, who happened to be one of the folks who invited me up to Othello, "Let's go catch those cows. That sure sounds like fun." He was up for some excitement so we loaded our horses and dogs and took off to the neighbor's property about three miles down the road.

When we got there we spoke to the owner of the cows who also happened to own a feed lot. I asked him about his cows. "Yeah, they're out there. I see them out in the fields all the time." He told me. "They're running with about thirty-five head but every time we bring them in, there's two that escape!" These 'fields' he's speaking of are thousands of acres! It's not like my place where I have something like five acres. Rounding up a few stray cows on my property is easy. Catching them on this guy's property is going to require skill and good dogs! I figure in order to catch these two renegade cows I'm going to have to bring the whole herd in, fight with the rowdy ones, and keep the two problem ones from slipping away.

We drove out a ways across those fields until we saw that herd of cows the owner described. They saw us and took off across an old gravel road. David and I quickly pulled over, unload the horses and cinched them up as fast as we could. We had to catch up to those cows. We knew it was going to be a problem bringing them in because of those two wild ones they hadn't been able to catch for something like three and a half years.

We decided to leave Sport in the truck because of the amount of distance we knew we'd have to cover and took my dog, Tyson instead. We rode out across the field toward the herd. I saw the feedlot owner sitting in his truck down the road watching us work. He had followed us out there to see what we were going to do.

David and I loped our horses across the field trying to angle these cows off. We got the herd to stop but two of them jumped the fence and were leaving. They were heading out across the sage brush. I had my horse Badger pointed in the direction the two cows went when I hollered at Tyson, "Get ahead"! He took off after them. David yelled over to me, "No man. Just let them go."

"No, we can get them." I yelled back. He just started laughing because he knew me well enough to know that I was going after those cows!

I wasn't able to follow after Tyson on Badger because of the barbed wire fence. The two cows ran off so far that I couldn't see Tyson anymore and could only catch a glimpse of the cows through the sage brush now and then. Soon enough l heard this cow bawling and I saw Tyson in the air! He'd grabbed the lead cow by the head and she was slinging him through the air! Tyson kept at her until she turned back toward the herd. The second cow kept running away from the herd.

David exclaimed, "He's got one turned!"

I could just see the cow that was running off and heading out across the fields. I hollered at Tyson to "On out" which meant for him to get ahead of her. By this time David had ridden up beside me to catch the action. Then I heard the second cow bawling in the distance.

"Man, he's got the other one!" I yelled!

"Are you serious?" David asked?

"Yeah, that cow will be back in a minute." And here they came. The second cow caught up to the first cow and both ran back and jumped the fence, with Tyson right on their heels!

David and I used our horses to get those two cows back with the herd. This whole incident took about five minutes. We started moving the herd toward the feed lot when this guy on his horse joins up with us. Just as we're almost back to the feed lot a fourth rider shows up and rides along! We thought we'd left everybody at the ranch but as the word got out about what we were doing, gathering up some difficult cattle, other people started showing up to see the action.

The herd was a bit wild so we ended up fighting with them for probably another 20 minutes. But eventually we got them back to the feed lot and started moving them through the gate. About this time another truck and trailer pulled up. I guess they wanted to help us too. They got their horse out and then let their dog loose. This dog ran into the middle of that herd of cows barking and yapping and fighting and all hell broke loose! Cows were running in every direction! I couldn't believe what I was seeing! David was so mad he practically turned red on the spot!

We'd been out there fighting and sweating and we finally had that herd right up to the gate of the corral when that dog about ruined the whole thing. Now the cows were going every which way! Tyson was pretty darn hot by then but I had no other choice than to send him back out, especially if we didn't want to lose those cows. In the meantime David was hollering at the people to put their dog up. Fortunately someone caught the dog and put him away. We fought these cows for a second time and eventually got them to the corrals and penned up.

We were pretty proud of ourselves after all this hard work! We rode over to the feedlot owner who was standing by the corrals with his binoculars hanging around his neck and figured he'd thank us for all our hard work and we'd be on our way but instead he said," You did great except for those two you didn't catch."

"What!" I was a little surprised to hear this. "What do you mean? They're in with that herd."

"Aw, no! They're still out there. I was sitting up here with binoculars watching you guys. Those two cows cut out in the sage brush and they went back across the fields."

"You're serious?" I asked him.

"Yeah, they're not here. They're definitely gone!"

I couldn't believe it but if he said he saw them leave I guess they're gone!

"All right then," I said to him, "I guess we'll have to get them."

David looked at me and asked, "What do you want to do?"

"Let's load up, man! Our dogs and horses are tired. We'll get them later." I'd had enough for now and Tyson needed a break. So we loaded everything up and headed back to the ranch.

Later that afternoon we were all sitting around the ranch talking when the ranch owner said, "We have a bull on the back part of the ranch that we wouldn't mind having caught. We haven't been able to catch him for awhile because we haven't been able to find him…he keeps brushing up."

I turned and said, "Shoot David, let's go get him."

So we loaded our horses, Tyson and Sport in the trucks and trailers and took off to find this bull. Joe came along with us. We drove to the field where the bull was last seen. We unloaded our horses, Tyson, and David's dog Josie and decided to leave Sport in the truck again. We rode out looking for this one bull on thousands of acres! We'd been riding for a little bit but weren't having any luck spotting him. Next thing I knew this bull jumped out from under the sage brush barely twenty feet in front of my horse! Poor Badger started blowing air through his nostrils hard; he was scared to death. He didn't know what this beast was coming out of the sage brush! Tyson was spooked too; he happened to be only about five feet away from the bull when it blew out of the brush.

The bull took off running down a hill away from us, went about three or four hundred feet then just laid down and crawled up under the sage brush!

"Holy Cow, I've never seen that before!" I said to David. "Do you think he's sick or hurt?"

"Man, I don't know."

We followed after him and got around behind where he was. Nobody wanted to get close to this thing. He was a big old bull who was acting very weird.

"I'm going to send Tyson in to get him out of that brush." I told David and Joe. When Tyson ran into the brush that bull came blowing out of there and took off again! Luckily, he was heading the right way. Our plan was to take him down the road a mile or two to some corrals and load him in the truck and trailer. He was heading the right way but I could tell he was going to get away from us. I sent Tyson ahead to slow him down.

This bull didn't want to slow down. He kept on going and going and going! We were slow loping our horses along behind him. We did this for about a mile before we finally got him to a fence on the back end of the property. He ran up to the fence then laid down in a bunch of old tumbleweed! He didn't want to get up! I was thinking 'What the heck!'

I said, "David, we're never going to get him through that gate and if we do we're going to lose him out in those big fields. What if they bring the truck and trailer over here? We'll load him right here. Want to give it a try?"

"Ok," David said, "Let's do it."

He got on his cell phone and called the guy with the truck and trailer and asked him to bring it over. About that time the bull decided to leave. He jumped up and took off back toward where he came from. I wasn't going to put up with any of this nonsense! I roped him and dallied him off to my saddle. My horse was not happy with this arrangement since he weighed about 1250 pounds and that bull probably weighed 1800!

As soon as I roped him I choked him down a little bit but he ran over to the tumble weeds and laid down in them again! Again I was thinking *'what the heck!'*

I told Tyson to "Get him up" and he ran over there and started biting on that bull's head. Of course the bull jumped up and wanted to kill my dog! Since they were in the tumbleweeds it put my dog at a real disadvantage so when the bull jumped up I called off Tyson. Tyson trotted back to me and right away the bull laid back down! I sent Tyson back to the bull, "Get him up!" Again Tyson latches on to his head. This went on four or five more times while I was waiting for the truck and trailer. Finally they drove up and asked me what I wanted to do.

"Back that trailer right up to this bull and open up that trailer gate." I told the folks with the trailer. "I'm gonna get that bull up and put him in the trailer." The folks were all laughing at me; I guess they just thought my idea was crazy but they did back the trailer up within fifteen feet of him.

"Okay. Open the trailer gate and back up a little bit closer. I had one of the guys on foot throw another loop on the bull and run it through that trailer and back out the side to my horse." I told one of the guys standing there. He moved in to do what I asked.

I sent Tyson behind the bull. I got my rope ready then told Tyson to "Get him up" and he jumped on the bull's head. As that bull leapt up in the air I hollered at Tyson to get out of there. I didn't want him getting hurt by that old bull. Unfortunately, Tyson ran right into the trailer and the bull followed right after him! I dallied my rope up real tight on my saddle horn and got the bull pulled up inside the trailer. About that time they slammed the trailer door shut…with Tyson inside! "Man, get my dog out of there!" I yelled. Someone opened the door and Tyson came shooting out of there as fast as he could. The trailer gate was quickly shut and securely latched.

It looked like I wasn't going to be able to get my rope off the bull. David said, "Just leave it on him."

"No way!" I cried, "That's a $75 rope! What if we see those two missing cows on the way back? I'm gonna need my rope for that."

There were four or five people out there by then. Everyone there started putting their arms, their sorting sticks or whatever else they could find, through the slats on the side of the trailer to help get the rope off the bull's head. It took us ten minutes but we got it off. I coiled the rope back up and put it on my horse.

We loosed the cinches on the horses and let them breath and rest for a minute after I got my rope. Then we rode back to where we left our truck and trailer. We loaded up and headed down the road back to the ranch. We were laughing and having a good time as we were cruising down these old gravel roads when all of a sudden I saw one of those missing cows in a small herd.

"There goes that cow! Park it now." I told David. He pulled over to the side of the road. I jumped out and the first thing I did was turn Tyson loose, pointed him in the right direction and told him to "Get ahead". Sport had been sitting in the truck this whole time not being able to do anything so I decided to turn him loose to help. I knew he wouldn't keep up but he could help out once we got that small herd stopped. "You ready David? Let's go get her. The feedlot owner offered me a hundred bucks if I catch the blue colored cow." I got my horse out and cinched him up. By the time David had his horse ready I was already taking off.

I guess there had been two cows and two older calves that had escaped from that big herd that we missed seeing. We were lucky that I spotted them when I did; we might actually have a chance at bringing them in! Tyson was able to stop them all about a half a mile away from us. We rode up to the cattle and I roped the blue cow which promptly charged my horse. She got her head between my horse's back legs and I was thinking she was probably going to kill me and my horse! Tyson was trying to help me so he went under my horse and started chewing on her head. David was screaming and hollering and I was just trying to stay alive at this point. The cow had enough of Tyson and finally got out from under my horse. I choked her down with my rope and got her lying on the ground. Now she'd really had enough; she didn't even want to move. I asked David if he could jump down and tie her feet together. He got off his horse and tied her feet up so she couldn't move. The feedlot owner, who just happened to be watching all of this through his binoculars, drove toward us on his four-wheeler.

"What now?" David asked.

"Do you think you can bring that front end loader around here? We'll just scoop her up in the bucket of the loader and you can take her back to the feed lot!" I said to the feedlot owner.

"Sure...but what about the other one?"

"What other one?" I jokingly said.

"The other cow!" He was serious.

"But you only offered me money for this one!"

We loaded that blue cow up in the front loader and I looked around for Sport but I didn't see him anywhere. I called for him but he didn't come.

Sport was ten years old and getting hard of hearing. His legs were bad and one ear was partly chewed off. But he was my buddy and he'd worked hard for me all these years. I was seriously worried about him so I had David and Joe help me look for him. We looked and looked but couldn't find him. Finally I had to give up for the time being so I could help deal with the cow.

When I stopped off at the feed lot, the owner gave me two one-hundred dollar bills for catching his cow! This was a nice surprise for me since I was only expecting one hundred.

"I'll give you another hundred if you can catch the other cow!" he told me.

"Ok, but I'll have to find my dog first." I was really worried about Sport because he should have shown up by then.

David, Joe and I started looking for Sport again. Pretty soon everybody at the ranch was looking for my dog. We couldn't find him. We keep looking for him until dinner time when we had to break for a quick bite to eat before we started looking again. I was really worried by this time. This was just not like Sport. We had to find him.

Eventually David and I took off in a gator so we could cover more ground. We looked everywhere. When it got dark we put the gator away and drove around in David's truck. We all kept searching until about eleven that night but still we couldn't find him. I headed back to the trailer, tired and saddened, to call my wife Jodi. I told her we couldn't find Sport. I just didn't know what I was going to do without that dog!

The next morning we were up at daylight. Before we went to gather cattle we all decided to look a little more for Sport. We rode back to where we last saw him. Pretty soon Joe hollered, "Hey, I see Sport out there with some cows."

"Naw…" I was looking real hard at where Joe was pointing, "He isn't out there with those cows. That's a calf out there."

"No man, I'm telling you, that's Sport. He's got all those cows held up against that fence. Just whistle for him."

Joe was pretty adamant so I whistled for Sport and sure enough, here comes this little black spot towards me…and it's Sport! He'd been out all night with these cows. They weren't even our cows; they were the neighbor's cows but I didn't want to tell Sport that and disappoint him! What was funny was I trained him to hold cows until I showed up and that was what he did; he held those cows all night long! Luckily there was some irrigation going so he had enough water during the night.

Sport came over to me and I petted on him for awhile. I wanted him to know what a remarkable dog he was! I knew I needed to take him back to the ranch so he could get some food and rest. As I was putting him in my truck I stated to the guys around me, "He's retired, that's it." I knew in my heart that this was mine and Sport's last cattle drive together. His loyalty and ability to follow my directions were what made him the best cow dog I ever owned.

Once we got back from that trip, I only used Sport around my place to play with the pups and help me out with their training. He never went on another cattle drive.

I will always have that picture in my mind of Sport holding those cows against that fence until he heard my call and came running towards me, so proud of himself for a good day's work. When I'm out riding the range in Othello, Washington I always remember Sport.

Chapter 45
The Blueberry Muffin
Spring 2010

My Blueberry Muffin tale all started because I got bored while gathering cattle on a ranch up in Washington. And like I've always said my boredom gets me into trouble because once I open my mouth I never like to fail!

We had loaded up our dogs and horses early that morning to gather a couple hundred cow-calf pairs and move them back to the ranch. I was riding my Quarter Horse Badger and using my cow dogs Tyson and Trap. Once the cattle were penned everyone started putting their horses up while they waited for lunch. While this relaxing was starting, I just happened to mention seeing a big, black Angus bull down in the field below the bunk house. One of the ranch owners was standing there and happened to overhear me make this remark. Right away he started saying how he sure would like to have that bull up in the corral but every time they've tried to catch him he goes down in the swamp by the creek and tall grass. So of course I asked if he would like for me to try and pen the bull. He said if I wanted to that would be great. So I woke Badger from his noon-time nap, cinched him up and called for my dog Tyson. I decided to leave Trap at the truck this time because I had a lot better handle on Tyson under these kinds of situations. I had a plan and it was going to be pretty simple, or so I thought.

A couple of the other guys who were there happened to hear I was headed out to get the Angus bull so they got their horses and took off down the field to help me. The problem was they didn't ask me how I wanted to approach this bull. I believe they thought this would be really easy, like they would just get around the bull real quick and drive him up and into the corrals. I had it figured to where Badger and I would go around to the left side of the bull and block him from the swamp. As I was getting ready to ride off, I saw this guy coming out of the big walk-in-cooler with a muffin in his hand. I hollered over to him asking if he had an extra one in there and he asked me what kind I wanted. I told him a blueberry one would be great. When he handed me my muffin I thanked him. Knowing where I was headed he just said good luck and started chuckling!

I started to peel the wrapper from my muffin as I headed down the hill on Badger. I had yet to actually get my muffin unwrapped when I saw two guys on horses going around the right side of the bull. About that time the bull saw these guys and took off for the swamp. I was still a good ways from him so I bumped badger with my boots and got him trotting while still trying to unwrap my nice smelling blueberry muffin. The bull made it to the edge of the tall grass and that was when I noticed Badger and I had stepped into a little water. I knew there was nothing to worry about because Badger had been in water a million times and this seemed shallow enough.

I could see I was losing the race to the creek where the bull wanted to cross. The good thing was I'd finally gotten the wrapper off my blueberry muffin and was ready to take a bite. As I put it up to my mouth, Badger stepped into what looked like a little stream. Suddenly he went down to his knees and sank to his belly in a deep bog! The blueberry muffin went flying from my hand and all I had left was a small pinch between my fingers! I couldn't believe it! And I was so hungry too; at least I was able to put that tiny pinch in my mouth and boy did it taste good!

At this point I had no blueberry muffin, the bull was across the creek and I had two guys with me who wanted to know what my plan was!

The first thing I told those guys was the bull wouldn't be over there and I would be eating my blueberry muffin if the two of them had asked what the plan was before riding off. Since they were with me now, I figured what the heck, let's go get the bull. I certainly didn't need to worry about dropping my blueberry muffin anymore.

We rode to get around the bull but he was too far out in front of us. He went all the way to the corner of the fence and was on the other side of two creeks now. The mud was so bad that there was no way I was going to try to get my horse over to where he was plus the grass down there was about 4 feet tall!

These two guys suggested I send Tyson over to get the bull out of the corner. I sat there thinking about this situation and how that was one big bull who happened to be in a really bad spot, especially for my dog.

These guys were really encouraging me to send in Tyson. I was trying to think this thing through because I knew it would be dangerous for Tyson. But I also knew Tyson and he lived for this kind of fight and a fight it would be! Even though that bull was about two thousand pounds and Tyson was only a 60 pound dog, I knew he could overpower him and I really wanted to get that bull in the corral.

I told Tyson to "Hunt him up" which meant go find the bull and bring him to me. Tyson took off and jumped into the first creek which was swift and deep. He swam across and as soon as he got on the other side we couldn't see him anymore because the grass was so tall and thick. I was guessing Tyson still had a couple of hundred yards to go since I wasn't sure where he was and I could just barely see the bull. The guys were now asking where Tyson was and I had no idea, all I could hear was the noise from the rushing stream. Finally I spotted the bull and in that moment I saw him drop his head like he was about to fight off something coming at him. I yelled out that Tyson had found the bull. Suddenly I saw Tyson slung through the air, heard the bull bellow and knew the fight was on! I started hollering at Tyson to "Bring him".

Those two guys were caught up in the moment now. They were yelling and hollering and doing a 'play by play' on how Tyson had the bull. All of us watched the bull moving back up the fence line the way he had come. Then he just stopped and wouldn't move. Again I was yelling at Tyson to "Bring him" and once again you could see that bull duck his head as he fought off the dog. Soon enough the bull started moving again. All three of us rode up our side of the creek and I told those two guys "Whatever you do don't try to move that bull or cut him off. Let me and Tyson do it. When I need help I'll tell you where to go!" This time they said they'd do what I wanted but I still made sure they stuck with me!

People love to watch Tyson work and those guys were getting to see Tyson at his best with this bull. It took Tyson about twenty minutes to get the bull back to where he was when I first saw him. I moved Badger around the bull to get him headed to the corrals on top of the hill. I asked the other guys to split up and help herd the bull up the hill. The bull finely figured it was a lot easier to just go with the flow and headed in the right direction. I kept Tyson back just enough to keep the bull moving. It took us another ten minutes before we had him in the corral. The two guys who rode with me started going on and on about how they had so much fun helping me and watching Tyson whip that bull.

Tyson was pretty hot and tired; he worked hard to get the bull brought in. I got off Badger and loosen his cinch then petted Tyson who was darn happy about the job he just did. That dog lives to work but once he was done he'd be happy to curl up in your lap and take a nap with you if you let him. There was only one thing that ruined a perfect ending to my day - I had gotten the last blueberry muffin that morning when I left to catch the bull!

Chapter 46
One Red Cow
Spring 2010

One fine spring a few years back I was up in Othello, Washington on a ranch working my cow dogs. My buddy David and I were out moving some cattle but we were also looking and watching for a cow the owner said he'd give us a hundred dollars if we could catch.

We moved the herd we were there for then loaded up our horses in the trailer and put the dogs in the back of the truck on their chains. As we were driving back to the ranch to call it a day we happened to see this hundred dollar cow along with two calves out in a field of sage brush. I told David to stop so we would catch her. We got Tyson out of the truck, unloaded our horses again and cinched the saddles up tight. We headed into the sage brush after this cow and of course she took off so I told Tyson to "Get ahead" and stop her. David and I took off after her on horseback but she was just crazy acting. She would not stop so we keep riding hard and eventually I lost David but I was determined to catch this cow. She was the last one from a herd we had caught a few days ago.

After about a mile or so Tyson got her stopped but the problem was she wouldn't let me get close enough to rope her. I was finally able to get within thirty feet of her but there was still some really tall sage brush between us. I saw that I would have to throw my rope over the sage brush and hope for the best. Tyson was giving me that look that said 'Man, don't miss! I don't want to fight her anymore!' I had my sixty foot ranch rope with me so I built a big loop and tossed it gently over the brush. It landed right on her head but she was looking straight at me so I couldn't jerk the slack without pulling it off her head. I was about to command Tyson to "Get her" so she'd turn her head but she suddenly dropped her head, the rope fell off and she took off again. I told Tyson to "Get ahead" again and took off after her. I coiled up my rope and nudged Badger into a lope after this cow. David still wasn't anywhere in sight.

After a few hundred yards Tyson stopped her once more. As I was trying to get close to her she took off. Once again I told Tyson to "Get ahead". I recoiled my rope and the chase was on. There was still no sign of

David. I was getting a little concerned about where he could be so I called him on my cell but he didn't answer. I was starting to think *'What am I going to do if I catch this cow? I'm not even sure where I'm at.'*

I was riding along following the dust cloud Tyson and the crazy, red cow were leaving behind. I rode for probably another half mile and by then my horse was so hot he'd lathered up. My dog was panting hard and his tongue was hanging out. Finally Tyson got the cow stopped and I was able to get within maybe twenty feet of her. See had managed to position herself on one side of the sage brush with me on the other side. Tyson was intently looking at me and I could just tell he was hoping I didn't miss again. I made a promise out loud to Tyson and my horse Badger, "Guys, if I miss this time and she runs, were done!" But boy, I sure hate to lose!

I built a big loop on my rope and leaned over the side of my horse so I could rope her around the sage brush. I threw my loop around the brush and it landed on her head. She was looking straight at me this time too. I told Tyson to "Walk up" to her. I was in luck since he was off to one side of her this time. When he moved she looked away from me and at him. I quickly jerked my slack up and the fight was on – kind of like fishing one giant catch! She was fighting hard to get out of that rope and bawling like crazy. I told Tyson to back off and he got out of the way fast. The cow fought me hard for a couple of minutes then just stopped. She stood there and stared at me. Now I wasn't sure what to do since I had no idea where I was and no idea where David was.

The cow was just quietly standing there looking at me so I got my cell phone out and called David. He finally answered.

"Hey man, where are you at?" I asked.

"Where am I at? Where the heck did you go? I've been looking all over for you!"

"You know," I started, looking all around me, "I have no idea where I'm at."

"Shesh Marvin, I gave up on that cow a long time back!"

"Well I'll tell you David," I said with a grin on my face, "one end of my rope is on that cow and the end is dallied off to my saddle."

"I can't believe it!" He sounded completely surprised.

"Well believe it! She's standing here staring at me." I mentioned again, "It's just that I don't know where we are…maybe 2 miles from where we started the chase?" I paused to look around some more, "There's this one big hill between me and the road and I'm close to the high lines."

"Just hang tight." David said. "I'm going to ride over this hill I'm near and see if it's the same hill you're talking about."

So Tyson and I, along with the cow, hung out for awhile and cooled off.

A few minutes later David called my cell and told me he was almost at the top of the hill he was closest to. While he was still on the phone I saw him and his horse crest the top of the hill I was looking at. He had another buddy with him and they both rode up to me laughing. I guess they thought I was plum crazy for going after this cow. I explained that there was actually a bounty on this cow and that stopped the laughing real quick as it dawned on them who was getting that money! We got a plan together so we could walk this cow to the gravel road and load her in a trailer. We started moving and it went well for about fifty feet before the cow decided she wanted to go the other way. We fought with her for about fifteen minutes when David finally said he was going to call the owner and see if he could get the loader out here for her in the field. The cow owner was darn happy we caught her and said he'd send a loader right out once David explained where we were. In the meantime I got the cow to lie down then David and his buddy tied her feet so she couldn't get up.

I stepped down from Badger, loosened the saddle and petted Tyson. While we were waiting on the owner with the loader I told David and his buddy all about the big chase and fight Tyson and I had with this crazy, red cow in order to catch her. As I was telling them what a great job Tyson did, how he helped me out so much, I felt like something was missing. That something was my dog Sport, and it was hard for me not to have him by my side. This was the first time in nine years that I had gone out cattle-catching without him. Luckily I had the next best thing; Tyson, his son.

The cow's owner showed up about thirty minutes later and we got that cow in the loader. The owner drove off with his cow back to his feed lot. David, his buddy and I rode back to our horse trailer. On the way I asked David if he thought they had any more cows they couldn't catch. He just started laughing at me.

When we got to the trailer we loaded the horses and Tyson then drove back to the ranch. We stopped at the feed lot where that hundred dollar cow was taken. The owner was sure happy to get her caught. He said she was going to the sale barn the next day. She'd been running loose for three and a half years! It sure felt good when I was done catching a cow and no one or animal got hurt. Everything was calm again and all was right with the world, at least for one cattle owner!

Chapter 47
Jim's Calves
August 2010

A friend of mine called one day and told me his buddy, Jim, had two loose calves he couldn't catch. He asked me to call him so a few minutes later I was introducing myself to Jim on the phone and asking him, "So, I hear you got some calves out. Are they dog-broke?"

"Yeah, the calves are out but they're not dog broke." He continued, "They just follow my truck or gator around when I got hay on the back...that's usually how I do anything with them."

"Well why don't you just throw some hay on your gator and go bring them in?"

"I would but they're not at home!"

As it turned out, Jim had rented some pasture and taken all his calves out there. He went to pick them up a few months later, backed up to the gate and thought they would all just go in his trailer. Fortunately for him, all of them did go in except two. They jumped the fence and left!

I told Jim, "I'm leaving tomorrow for Othello, Washington for a cattle gathering so I don't have much time. Do you know where they are?"

"I think so," he said.

"I can load up and come over real quick. Do you have horses you can use so you can ride out with me or do I need to bring some extras?"

"Oh yeah, I got horses."

"Okay then. I'll come right over." I loaded up my horse, Badger and my dogs, Sport, Chic, and Tyson and drove to Jim's house. The plan was to meet him there then follow him out to the property.

I arrived at Jim's house and he had a trailer loaded with two big, stout horses and a buddy there. He told me they both planned on riding out with me to help.

I followed them in my truck to Dundee, the next town over, then a little outside of town to the property. Once we parked I started unloading the horses, dogs, and gear. I asked Jim, "Do you rope?"

"Nope...sorry." I was hoping that one of those guys could rope in case we had to rope both cows. I figured I'd just have to make do with one roper - me!

"Okay, well let's go see if we can find those calves. So do you know where they are?"

Jim pointed to his left out across the property. There was no sign of any calves as far as the eye could see. "I think they're down over there."

We rode for about two hours but we couldn't find any calves.

"You know what Marvin, I'll sell you those two calves cheap." I could tell frustration was setting in.

"How much do they weigh," I asked.

"About 900 pounds or so."

"Well, I would like to buy them but I don't want to buy them if we can't find them!"

This of course made sense to Jim so we continued our search. Eventually I had to call off the search because I had to go home and pack for my trip to Othello. I apologized to Jim for leaving a job without completing it. While I was loading up I told Jim, "While I'm gone you just keep an eye out for those calves. Ask the neighbors to call you if they happen to see them. I'm probably going to be gone three days."

On the second day I was up in Othello I got a phone call from Jim.

"We spotted them!" He sounded pretty excited.

"Okay, that's great! Just don't chase them. Leave them alone. They should have plenty of grass and water. When I get back, we'll go get them."

As soon as I got back from Othello I called him. "Do you know where they are?"

"Yup, we know where they are."

I let him know I'd be out the next day and we'd catch them this time. The next morning I got my dogs, horse, ropes, and trailer ready and took off to meet Jim where he said the calves were located.

The first thing I said when I showed up was, "Where are they?"

"Well, I'm not sure" Jim muttered.

"You're kidding? I thought you had them spotted?"

"Well I did." He said then explained, "They were here last night. People saw them but I don't know where they are now."

"All right..." I sighed then said, "We'll start looking."

Jim, his buddy, and I rode around for a few hours. We checked with the neighbors or anyone around who might have seen them. No one had seen them since yesterday.

For some reason I got this gut feeling they were down at the old airstrip at the end of Dundee somewhere in the brush. We rode over there to look but still couldn't find them.

"Jim, they have to be down in that brush. That's the only place they can be." I was just sure of this. I continued with my train of thought, "The only trail I see is down that airstrip into the brush. They're going there to bed down and the only time they're coming up to eat is when no one's around. Walk down in there and I'll hold the horses. I'll keep my dogs and my horse ready and if they come up out of there we'll get them caught."

Jim followed the trail into the brush. Soon he started yelling, "They're here, they're here!"

I hollered to him, "Come back out and tie your horse up! Then take Sport back there with you and I'll keep Tyson and Chic up here with me. When you get down there just tell Sport to 'Get 'em'. If the only way out is this way, he'll bring them out."

Jim ran out, tied his horse up then quickly dashed back into the brush with Sport at his heels. Soon enough I heard Jim yelling "Get em", then Sport barking and pretty soon the cows were stomping and popping up through the brush. I sent the other two dogs over and the three of them got those calves bayed up.

One of the things you have to know when you work dogs on cattle is if you get the dogs to stop them, you want to stay way back. You don't want to get too close to the cattle because you'll scare them off. I was sitting a ways back on my horse but forgot to tell Jim about this little piece of advice. He rode right up to those two calves and they immediately split up and took off! Right away I called the dogs to me and took off after one of them. I chased this calf all the way down a gravel road, managed to get him turned and headed him right back to the corral he escaped from. I was pretty happy for that bit of good luck. I quickly shut the gate. He could see some other calves in a field across the driveway so he was feeling comfortable and calm.

I rode back down to Jim and asked him, "Where did the other one go?"

"I think he went right back down where he came from, right in the brush." He told me and pointed.

"Okay, we're going to try the same plan. You go back down in there with Sport and sic him on that calf and when he comes out of there I'll try to get a rope on him."

I was sitting right by the trail with Tyson and Chic beside me. I heard Jim yell again and Sport barking. Pretty soon the barking sounded like it was getting farther from me. *'Dang, that cow is going the other way.'* I muttered to myself. I saw the calf cutting through the brush in the other direction. I sent Chic and Sport after him but kept Tyson with me. I rode around the brush followed the calf. The calf went up this gravel road and turned left, went onto another gravel road, turned again and was pointed straight for the town of Dundee!

Sport and Chic were having trouble stopping him and I was just loping my horse, with Tyson beside me, behind them. I waited until the calf with the two dogs running beside him came alongside a nearby field then I told Tyson, "Get ahead". Tyson shot out toward the calf and now he had three dogs chewing on him. They slowed him down to a trot and he turned into the field. He was just walking now because the dogs were fighting with him pretty hard. I rode up close with my horse, threw a loop over his head and dallied him off to my saddle.

About that time Jim came racing up the side road on his horse. I was telling the dogs to bring the calf up behind me as I led him back to the corral. The dogs keep the calf moving along nicely.

Jim asked, "What do you want me to do?"

"Just hang back a ways if you don't mind." I told him, remembering the last time he got too close to the calves.

We got down to the big lot where the truck and trailer were parked. I was holding this calf with my horse and dogs when Jim and his buddy caught up.

"What now?" Jim asked.

"Just open that trailer gate. I bet this calf wants in that trailer!"

Jim opened the trailer gate and the calf ran inside as fast as he could. He couldn't wait to get away from my dogs.

"You know what, Marvin?" Jim started saying, "I thought this cattle hunting was about the boring-est thing I've ever done until we found them. Man, then everything just went crazy!"

"Yeah, I know. That's the way it normally is."

"So what do you want to do with the calf that's in this corral?"

"I'm not sure." I told him. I paused to think for a moment then continued, "I think I'll rope him and tie him to that tree over there." I pointed to a tree right outside the corral. Then you can back the trailer up to the gate. I'll just dally the rope on my horse and we'll pull him in the trailer."

The calf in the pen was now going snot-blowing crazy because of all the noise and commotion in the lot. I finally got a rope on him and tied him to the tree while we moved the trailer to the corral.

We put the calf in the trailer up toward the front then opened the divider. It took us another five minutes to get the second calf into the trailer and shut the gate.

"Whew! I can't believe it! We're done!" Jim exclaimed.

"Well, the thing is," I explained to Jim, "...always have good corrals to load from. You just have a regular old wire fence holding these cattle in. When you gathered up your herd of cattle to load them and bring them home, these two runaway calves saw the ones across the road and that's where they wanted to go and so that's where they went! There wasn't a good corral to hold them in."

"Yeah, I see that now! Thanks a lot Marvin," Jim said, "I appreciate all your hard work."

We went back up to my truck to load the horses. The neighbors happened to be out watching us work with these two calves. As I rode by them, they told me how they couldn't believe this kind of stuff could be done with dogs. Maybe they'd seen cattle gathering on some Western show but most of those you never really saw a dog helping with the cattle. If you have good dogs it makes catching cattle a whole heck of a lot easier. Jim was glad to have his cows back home and I was glad to have helped!

Chapter 48
Just One Bull
Summer 2010

I was hanging out one day, not doing much of anything, when I got a call from my friend Wiley. He asked me if I would like to go catch a bull for him.

As usual I asked how much the bull weighed and where he was located. Knowing Wiley I figured it was probably an old roping bull and it would be a challenging job. He told me the bull weighed about 700 to 800 pounds and he was in Molalla. I said I could be there within a couple hours. I hooked up the trailer and got Badger saddled up. I loaded him into the trailer then got my dogs Tyson and Trap out of the kennels and put them in their dog boxes on the back of the truck.

I made arrangements to pick Wiley up on my way out to Molalla. He decided he wasn't going to bring a horse on this trip. I was sure hoping we didn't have to chase this bull halfway across the country because there was no way I was packing Wiley on the back of Badger!

We drove to Molalla and on the way Wiley told me that the bull was down by the barn the last he saw him. They had loaded the herd of cattle the bull was with but instead of him joining them in the trailer, he jumped the fence and ran off. I knew from experience that once cattle got into this habit of jumping fences, it was hard to catch them and even harder to break them from jumping fences whenever they had pressure on them.

When we finally arrived at the property and the barn, the bull was nowhere in sight. We decided I should just pull into the field and unload my horse and dogs anyway, just to be ready. The plan was for Wiley to walk across the field and see if the bull was in the barn. If so, he would run him out and I would wait until he got in the field. Then I would have the dogs either stop him or slow him down enough where I could rope him.

Wiley no sooner disappeared into the barn when out shot this bull as planned. I waited for him to get closer to me in the field then I sent the dogs after him. They slowed him to a trot and I brought Badger up alongside him. I told the dogs to back off so I could throw a loop of rope around his head. Unfortunately I missed. The bull took off so I hollered at the dogs to "Get ahead". They slowed him down once more. By this time he was near the trailer. I threw my rope at him and this time I caught him. Boy was he mad! I guess he thought he'd gotten away!

I had the dogs bring him up from behind as I rode the short distance to the trailer leading him from my horse. When we were at the trailer I lean over and opened the back gate. I had the bull out on about 40 feet of rope. I told the dogs to bring him toward the trailer and the fight was on. The dogs lit into that bull the moment he protested going toward the trailer but after a minute he reconsidered, ran around my horse and straight into the trailer. I jumped off my horse and shut the trailer gate. I gave all the dogs a pet and told them what a good job they had done!

Wiley came walking up from the barn and asked where the bull was. I told him he was in the trailer hiding from the dogs. Wiley was surprised at what quick work that was and we both had a good laugh over it. Together we got the rope off the bull, shut him in the front part of the trailer, loaded the dogs up and drove back to the ranch. Catching that bull took probably 30 minutes. It took us longer to drive out there and back than to catch him. Cattle gathering days like this one are always a blessing!

Chapter 49
Four Little Calves
September 2010

I sure like it when people call me to gather their cattle. Not too long ago I started gathering bucking stock. Now that's really fun! Those animals don't know fences were built to keep them in. The cows seem to start teaching their calves to jump fences as soon as they're born!

My dogs, because they're well trained, can usually handle these ornery calves so most of the time we don't have too many problems. This occasionally leads to being over confident with my dogs and that's when I end up learning some important lessons!

One day a guy I know named Ken called wanting me to help him catch four calves. I thought to myself, 'four calves? NO PROBLEM!' I arranged to meet Ken the next day which happened to be a day before I went elk hunting. I loaded my horse, Badger, and my two best dogs, Hangin' Tree Sport and Chic, and drove out to meet Ken. When I got there we easily trapped the adult cows and the bull with grain but the four calves were having none of it! They were not about to come into the pen.

We decided to go ahead and load the cows and bull then work on getting the calves caught. Thinking back, I'm not sure why I attempted to bring the four calves into a half moon-shaped pen with only a little four foot walk-through gate in the middle. I had made that half moon-shaped pen more inviting to the calves by leaving one cow in a little separate pen inside it. The reasoning being that usually if calves see other cows they want to be with them. Boy was I wrong!

As it turned out I could stop the calves with my two dogs but couldn't get them into the pen. Finally I was able to get one of the calves in the pen but then she tore it down and got out! I started chasing those calves with my horse but then my horse went down in a spring and that ended that!

By this time we were all worn out; me, my horse, and my dogs. I told Ken that we needed to quit since it was getting dark anyway. This meant that we had to unload the cows and bull back into the pasture since we hadn't caught those four calves. After that I headed for home feeling somewhat defeated. I don't like it when I can't accomplish something I set out to do; especially gathering calves.

When I got back from elk hunting I called Ken to see if he had any luck penning up his calves. He hadn't had any success on his own so I asked him if he was ready to give it another shot.

We set it up differently this time. We started out at 10:00 am on a Sunday so we would have plenty of daylight hours to work with. I also asked my son Jason if he wanted to come along and help which of course he did. He knows we always have a good time gathering cattle.

That Saturday night I didn't get much sleep because I was thinking about those four little calves. This time they weren't going to get away!

We met Ken and his wife on Sunday morning and Ken asked me how I wanted to go about catching the herd and especially those four little wily calves! I told him we'd open a big 12 foot panel off the pen, angle it out, and then I'd send my two dogs out to hold up the cattle. There were about five or six cows, the four calves I couldn't catch, and one big bull in the whole group.

The dogs balled up the cattle and once they settled down a little, Ken dumped grain into the feeders. I then had the dogs move the cattle into the corral. Some of them went straight in but there were a few that wanted nothing to do with the corral. Each time I got them close they tried to get around it but Sport and Chic would get them stopped. This lasted about two minutes. Finally they all went into the corral. Some of those cows didn't want to stay in that corral. They kept pushing against the panels to try to bust their way through but Sport and Chic would bite on their heads and push them away from the panel sides. The calves didn't even try and run; they had had enough the last time they meet those two dogs!

We shut the one panel but a couple of the cows headed to the back side of the corral hoping to bust their way out. I sent Chic around the outside of the pen and one look at that dog biting through the bars at their heads got them stopped!

The herd settled down nicely and the whole process took maybe fifteen minutes.

What I learned from those little calves is that you should really think about what kind of dog power you have and set up the situation so you can win! I had plenty of dog power but I should have opened up a panel and brought the whole herd in at one time. I could have gotten all four calves in if I would've done that. Because of my mistakes I thought about those four darn little calves the whole time I was hunting! I was supposed to be concentrating on getting an elk!

The thing about working dogs with cattle is that you'll probably make mistakes; the key is just trying to learn from them.

Chapter 50
You Don't Need Your Horse
Fall 2010

Many times when I've gone to gather cattle the owners will tell me that I don't need to bring my horse. They'll tell me their cattle will come at the rattle of a grain bucket and not to worry that they're on a few hundred acres! Well, I thought I had learned my lesson with this a while back but on this particular day what did I do? I left my horse at home!

It started with a phone call from a lady who wanted me to bring my dogs and help pen some cows ASAP. She also wanted me to haul a load to the sale barn. We set a day and time to pen her cows and she assured me that it'd be super easy and I wouldn't need my horse.

On the day I went to gather this lady's cattle, I hooked up my trailer and got Sport and Chic from their kennels. I loaded them in their dog boxes on the back of my truck and against my better judgment I left my horse Badger at home.

When I drove up to the property I was greeted by a man who had no idea where everyone was as he was the only one there! He told me where to park and once I'd stepped out of the truck I started looking around for the cattle.

Finally I saw some cows but they were surely not the ones I was here to pen and haul away because, heck, they were way down in a field at the bottom of the big hill I was parked on. After wandering around and not finding any other cows, the lady who called me showed up, followed by a few more people.

We were all standing around talking and meeting one another when I got around to asking her where the cattle were. She said in the field and pointed down the hill to those little black specks dotting the distant landscape. Right then I was mentally kicking myself for not bringing Badger. However, one of the guys that showed up with this lady said it shouldn't be a problem because he had a four-wheeler.

Before starting off we set some panels up so we could corral the cattle and load them into the trailer. When everything was ready we walked down this big hill to gather the cattle out of the very large field. It went about as I expected it would; the cattle did not want to go up the hill to the barn. So we were down there with one guy on a four-wheeler and he was zipping around everywhere but we really needed four more of these four-wheelers to even begin accomplishing the task of gathering up these cows; or I at least needed my horse. The thing was we had neither.

We kept working and chasing these cattle for about another hour until we finely got them up the hill and into the corral, an exhausting job! I mentioned to the lady that I knew at least two of the cows weren't in the pen because they ran by us in the blackberries. She said that was okay because they'd just get them later. So without too many more problems I loaded one bunch of cows in my trailer and another in the lady's trailer. Then we drove off to the sale barn. Once we'd finished with business at the sale barn this lady told me not to worry about the other cows that ran off, she'd get them caught and loaded when they come into the barn to eat. We parted ways with her laughing and promising she'd never tell me I wouldn't need my horse again. I drove home, sore and tired from chasing cows up and down a giant hill on foot.

About two weeks later this lady called me saying they had a cow, one bull, and a couple of calves trapped in a corral but they couldn't get close to them because they kept trying to tear the panels down. She asked if I could bring my dogs over and help load them and haul them to the sale barn. We made arrangements to haul them the next morning because she was worried they were going to bust out of the corral if she waited too long.

The next morning I got up early to do my chores and all the while I was thinking about how to get this cattle job done the safest and easiest way. It was one of those things you can think about all day and it doesn't do any good until you're there and see what the setup looks like.

I hooked up the trailer and loaded Sport and Chic. When I got to the property this lady and some of her friends were there. They said the cattle were going crazy and trying to tear down the corral panels. I was curious why they were so wild until someone told me they had never been locked in a corral before.

They wanted me to walk over and look at the situation first so I could figure out what to do. I told them there really was no need since I'd been there before and I knew exactly where I needed to park and how to set it up. I pulled into the barn lot and backed up to the corner of the corral. When I got out of the truck and walked back to the trailer to open the gate the old cow in the group charged the panels and hit them hard. I could see she had one bad attitude. Everyone nervously laughed and said they warned me.

There was no way to get into the corral to set up any panels and besides, we didn't have any extra panels to begin with. So I explained to the folks there how I was going to open up one of the panels and point it toward my trailer then send my dogs into the corral to see if they couldn't encourage the cattle to jump into the trailer.

I unloaded Sport and Chic. I told a person standing near the back of the trailer to get ready and shut the trailer gate when the cattle loaded.

I sent the dogs into the corral and as soon as they set foot under those panels that old cow came charging at them. When she reached the dogs they both jumped on her head and started biting. She didn't like that biting one bit so she backed off but then charged another panel in an attempt to break out. Luckily the panel held so she charged my dogs again. I could tell this pattern was not going to work for too long. Eventually either my dogs or the panels were going to give!

Any time I get into a situation like this I have to try and figure out a way to keep my dogs as safe as possible. In this particular situation the best way would have been to leave and get more panels. But I was thinking that if I left, the cattle might tear their way out and be gone by the time I got back so that wasn't going to work. I needed another tactic.

I decided to redirect my dogs toward the bull and two calves as they were a little easier to deal with. I had them put the bull and calves in and out of the trailer maybe ten times. I didn't shut them in because I wanted that old cow to see them in there and maybe follow. I worked my dogs on the bull and calves for awhile then let them rest so that old cow could think things over. After about thirty minutes the cow decided to just walk into the trailer. The fight was over.

As I was closing the trailer gate the lady and her friends were telling me how well my dogs listened and how great they were. It sure was a nice feeling when I latched the trailer gate and inside were the cows I had come to catch!

Chapter 51
Loose Cows on Highway 47
Gaston, Oregon
December 2010

It all started with a phone call from Jon; some cattle were loose and running around on Highway 47 near Gaston, Oregon. This of course was never a good thing!

Jon said he was headed that way with a stock trailer and needed my help. I asked him if he needed me to bring my dogs and horse. "Sure," he said. I loaded up my Quarter Horse, Badger, and my dogs; Tyson and two of my Hangin' Tree Cowdogs.

When I showed up in Gaston there were a few Yamhill County and Oregon State Police Officers milling about. I was told by the officers that there were three head of cattle down in the brush at the edge of the field and no one could do anything with them.

About that time Jon called me from down in the field. He was trying to keep the cattle from moving into a bigger field at the edge of the smaller one. He asked me what I wanted to do just as I was asking him what he wanted to do! I suggested that we have the road blocked by ODOT (Oregon Department of Transportation) who had shown up by that time. I told the police officers that I would ride down into the field with Tyson to see if he could control the cattle. We would try to bring them up to the road and load them into Jon's trailer since we couldn't get the trailer into the field.

As soon as I rode down there the cattle brushed up. This was going to make it difficult for me to rope any of them. I could see that the only option I had was to send a dog into the brush to bring them out into the smaller field. I told Tyson to go "Get 'em". He darted into the brush and you could hear the fight going on between dog and cows! There was barking and bawling and I could see one cow go for Tyson like it was going to kill him or at least run him off!

Tyson fought it out with the cow and calves for awhile before the cow and one calf came out of the brush and up to the road. I stayed down in the field on my horse where I could keep an eye on the other big calf that was still in the brush. I thought I might have to rope the two that came out and tie them to trees to keep them from running off. Then I decided it would be better, and a lot less work, if I brought them back into the field. I wasn't going to be able to move the one calf by itself because I knew if I brought it out of the brush it'd just panic without the other ones near and run off. I needed to move them all as a group.

I told Tyson to bring the two back into the field. Tyson ran up to the road and I could hear the fight going on between him and the cow and calf. After a few minutes the cow and calf came running back into the field and I got Tyson to bring them near the lone calf. By then Jon was backing his truck up to where the two cattle had come out onto the highway. He set up a couple of panels to help guide them into the trailer. All three cattle were out of the brush now so I had Tyson help me head all three of them out to the road. Once we got out there the cow kept trying to get around the panels and into the berry bushes. I roped her and drug her back to the trailer. I had Tyson hold the calves until Jon got a couple more panels set up. Tyson and I had all the cattle on the road by the back of the trailer. The cow started into the trailer but all of a sudden she stopped! Luckily Tyson bites when I tell him to. He bit the cow and she immediately jumped into the trailer with the two calves following close behind. We shut the gate and it was over!

I have learned over the years that when people don't know about me, my dogs, and the services I offer they can end up chasing their cattle for days and sometimes weeks until the only option left is to call the slaughter truck and have their cattle shot. Then they have to move the bodies, store the meat, find buyers and so on. It's a lot easier to just contact me. I'll come on out with my horse and dogs, catch the cattle usually within a day and everyone ends up happy and alive.

Chapter 52
CeCe Jumps Out
Spring 2011

I gather a lot of cattle for a roping arena near where I live in Newberg, Oregon. On one of these occasions Wiley, the guy who runs the arena, called me for some help catching cows that were located on two different properties. One was out by Molalla and one was near where I lived. Wiley said he'd meet me out in Molalla.

I loaded up my horse Badger and my dogs Tyson and Cece and drove out to meet Wiley and help him catch some cattle. Cece was a young dog and I didn't like working her all that much. I had bought her as an older pup and she wouldn't really work for either me or my wife. But that day I took her with me figuring I'd try to work her with another dog and see if that made a difference.

When we arrived at the Molalla property I pulled Tyson out and decided not to work Cece. I was in such a great mood I just didn't feel like spoiling it with an uncooperative dog. I rode up this hill on Badger and with Tyson's help managed to get the cattle out of the brush and down to the corrals. It probably took us all of about 20 minutes. We loaded the cattle into Wiley's trailer. I put Badger back in my trailer, up in the front section then put the dogs in the back section of the trailer like I always do. They were loose and not tied to anything, again like I have always done.

I followed Wiley back to the other property that was near where I lived. We were driving down the road doing the speed limit which was 45. We arrived at the property and Wiley pulled into the entry way to the pasture. I was sitting in my truck in the road, waiting for Wiley to open the pasture gate so I could drive in, when this guy pulled up behind me in his truck and came running up to my window.

"Did you have a dog on the back of your truck?" He asked.

"No sir, I have two in the back of my stock trailer though."

"Well…now you only have one. I saw one jump out back down the road a ways."

I jumped out of the truck and ran around to the back of the trailer. I opened the gate and saw Tyson lying there contentedly but Cece was gone!

I was looking at the area they were in and couldn't figure out where she'd gotten out until I looked up and noticed the six inch wide open slats on the side of this stock trailer near the top. The only thing I could figure was she climbed the side of the trailer wall and crawled out the small opening!

"Thanks, I appreciate you letting me know." I told the guy, then asked, "By the way, can I get you to give me a ride back down the road to get her?" With the truck and trailer and horse and dogs in it, it'd just be a lot easier if I could get that guy to give me a ride back to pick up CeCe. The guy was very obliging but unfortunately his truck wouldn't start and here we were, all parked in the middle of the road! I hollered up to Wiley, "One of my dogs jumped out. Take Tyson and go ahead and gather the cows. I'll run back down the road with this guy and get my dog."

I had to back my truck and trailer up in the middle of the road and give this guy a jump. Then I parked my rig alongside of the road and got in this guy's little truck.

"Do you know where she is?" I asked him as I sat down.

"I know exactly where she is. She is six point four miles up the road! I marked it on my odometer so I would know exactly where I saw her." This was a good thing, at least I didn't have to spend half the day searching for a missing dog.

We cruised back up the road to the spot he saw her jump out.

"She was right here when I left her. She wouldn't come to me. I tried to call her. I was just going to put her in my truck and bring her to you but she wouldn't come to me."

I called her a couple of times and soon enough she came running out of this little Christmas tree farm. She had a couple scratches on her but that was it. The guy told me she had jumped out of the right side of my trailer which was a good thing because it meant she had landed in a ditch full of grass instead of on the gravel! I picked her up and put her on the front floor board of the truck and the guy took us back to my rig. I thanked him and offered to pay him but he wouldn't take any money.

"Well, thanks again," I said, "I sure appreciate it."

I carried CeCe back up to my truck and tied her in the back. Then I went walking out in the pasture looking for Wiley. I found him out there walking around in one of the fields with Tyson by his side.

"Have you caught the cows?" I hollered over to him.

"This dog won't work for me. Tyson won't work a lick for me!" then he laughed.

"Let me grab my horse and I'll come out there and get them." I pulled Badger out of the trailer and rode him into the field. It took me and Tyson five or ten minutes to get the cattle and put them in the corrals.

"Man, is CeCe all right?" Wiley asked me when I was done gathering the cattle.

"She's fine. I'm not sure why she bailed out of my trailer. I can't believe that!"

Wiley was going to come back later and load up the cattle so we both made our way back to our trucks.

I made sure Cece was securely tied up this time! In all my years of working cow dogs I never had one that jumped out of a trailer going down the road. Especially one that climbed the wall and crawled out a window to do the jumping! That was a first!

Chapter 53
How to Make Your Day
a Lot Shorter and Easier!
June 2011

There are times when I don't get to work my dogs as much as I would like because I own a fencing business and it's what I typically do to earn a living. But anytime I get a chance, I help people gather their cattle.

One summer my neighbor asked for my help hauling four loads of cows and calves and one load with a bull for a total of five loads. I knew it would be some good work for my dogs so I showed up at his place figuring I was in for a smooth and easy day.

My first problem was I didn't take a horse with me and being on foot with this many cattle wasn't a good thing! The second problem was not all of the corrals were opened and it ended up being a fight to get some of the young calves into those corrals because there weren't enough openings!

There must have been 50 head of cattle; some of them Charolais crosses who love to put up a fight! Good thing I had Hangin' Tree Tyson and Hangin' Tree Trap with me. It only took about ten minutes with those dogs to get the cattle all penned up and then only a short amount of time to sort out the cows and calves we didn't want hauled.

We loaded the trailer and left about six big calves for the next load. I noticed when we were leaving that the main gate out to the fields had one of those cheap chain and latch combos. Well I knew we had enough bailing twine lying around to reach to the moon and I should have used some of it to secure the gate but I was in a hurry so I decided not to worry about it.

We dropped off the first load of cattle, picked up another load and delivered them to the sale barn. Then we picked up a calf from another friend's house on the way back.

When all that was done we made our way back to my neighbor's property. As we drove into the barn I turned to my neighbor and asked him if all those calves in the field were supposed to be there! Well of course they weren't. Right then I knew what had happened. They had pushed open a poorly secured gate! I should have used that twine to secure the gate!

The only ones that were happy to see those calves loose were Tyson and Trap. Fortunately it only took those dogs about five minutes to get the calves back through the open gate and penned.

The lesson: Remember to secure your gates or else make sure you have some really great cow dogs with you!

During this same busy week I got a call asking me if I wanted to go pen about 60 head of roping steers. Of course I couldn't pass up an opportunity like that to work my dogs! I loaded up a couple horses and my dogs, and picked up my friend Nathan on the way so he could videotape the whole event. I had another friend, Stacey, waiting to help me and to ride my other horse.

We drove for about an hour to reach the place only to find out the steers weren't dog broke. Fortunately I had brought along Tyson and Trap who were seasoned cow dogs. I also brought Dottie who was the offspring of Sport and Chic. She was only two years old and had never been on a cattle gathering like this so it was definitely an education for her.

Surprisingly it only took about 30 minutes to get the roping steers out of the brush and into the barn even with inexperienced Dottie along!

I felt pretty good. I was thinking everything had gone smoothly enough and that we were all done with a short day of work.

Stacy and I tied our horses back at the trailer; I put Dottie in the dog carrier, and told Tyson and Trap to stay under the truck.

We started back to the barn on foot to help load the steers when someone hollered, "The steers are busting out and heading for the hills."

I knew I was the last one through the barn lot gate and then it dawned on me that I might also know who left the gate open! I hollered for Tyson and Trap as I ran into the lot. I got there just in time to witness a mass of steers going through the gate. I told my dogs to "Get ahead". They raced up to the lead steer but he wouldn't stop. They hit him again and again. By this time they were a couple hundred yards out of the lot so I went back for my horse and Dottie. I yelled at Stacy to get the other horse as I took off after the herd.

It wasn't looking good. I didn't think the dogs were going to get the steers stopped before they got to the brush and hills. I was running at a pretty good clip on my horse after them. I had gotten about 400 yards when I saw the steers come back around a corner straight at me with the dog's right behind them! The steers saw me in front of them and started turning on my dogs. I knew if my dogs could have talked I would have gotten a good cussing. It took a few minutes before we got them headed the right way. And I got out of the way! Good thing the dogs were so skillful.

My dogs were hot and tired after that fiasco. When we finally got the steers in the corral it was time for the dogs to cool off and drink some water.

We didn't have the best set up with the corrals so it took us another two hours to get all those steers in the barn again.

Once again, time and effort could have been saved if there had been a secure gate – and a shut one!

Chapter 54
A Trip to Washington
Summer 2011

One summer day this fellow named Phil contacted me through my website about working with his dog. He wanted me to work her on cattle and assess her herding abilities. After talking to Phil a little we made a plan for him to bring his dog out to me the following week.

When he showed up with his dog we started off by working some of my dogs first before giving his dog an opportunity to work the cattle. I quickly surmised that I'd need to work her a bit more than this one day for me to give a fair evaluation. So we agreed I would keep her a couple of weeks. Once those weeks were up Phil wanted me to bring her to his son's place in Washington. He was interested in having me meet his son and for me to see his son's cattle operation. I was told I could even work some of his son's cattle to show off my dogs' abilities.

When the two weeks were up and I was making plans to head to Washington, I called a buddy of mine, David, who lived near where I was going and asked if he wanted to meet up with me to do some riding and work dogs. He was very agreeable to the idea. So I got Badger and his equipment ready, hooked my trailer up and picked Tyson and Trap to take along. Once I was all loaded up I drove to Washington.

I met up with David and his wife Julie a few hours after crossing over into Washington from Oregon. They followed me in their truck and trailer the last few hours before reaching Phil's son's house.

When we arrived, introductions were made all around and everyone got to talking. I could quickly tell from what the son was saying that he felt he didn't need or want a dog. I told the son there was no need for me to work my dogs on his cattle then because there was no sense in me taking a chance of getting them hurt if he wasn't even interested in what they could do. We were all standing around talking when Phil reminded his son about his bull across the road that he hadn't been able to catch for some time. The son told us there was just no way to load him in a trailer, especially where he happened to be located. I asked if we could get a trailer into the field and at least close to where the bull was hanging out and I was told it was possible though not too close. I asked how big the bull was and they told me about eleven hundred pounds. I said we should be able to get him caught if we could find him. David had brought his dog along too so I knew we had the dog power to get him bayed up.

The next morning we all loaded up and headed across the main road. Then we drove across the fields for awhile before stopping. I was told we'd have to ride our horses from that point on.

The son proceeded to tell me he thought the bull would be about a quarter of a mile straight ahead. So David, his wife Julie, and I all got our horses ready and the dogs out. Once we started riding David asked me what the plan was.

"This bull has a lot of country to move around in," I told David, "So, if we find him I want to get a rope on him as soon as I can. I don't want to try and bring him back to the trailer without roping him because if he runs into the timber we're in trouble. It'll be really hard to get him out of there." David agreed with me. I knew the dogs could stop the bull in the timber but boy would it be hard to move or get to him.

We kept riding but there was all this electrified cross-fencing everywhere so the son had to come along with us on foot to take some of it down so we can get through. After riding for about 30 minutes we spotted the bull. He was standing on a little hill by a creek and there was a lot of brush around him.

I told David, "I'm going to ride over to where he is and have my dogs get his attention." My plan was to get a rope on him then figure out how to get him out of there. As I rode toward the bull he started eye-balling me. I got to within 30 feet of him and I could see he was getting nervous and about to run. I knew once I picked my loop up I'd have to throw quick or I'd lose him. I can usually move Tyson a few inches at a time towards cattle so I got my loop ready and told Tyson to watch him. I told Trap to stay. Once my loop was ready I had Tyson walk up real slow. As soon as that bull moved I swung one time, threw and told Tyson to "Down!" all at the same time. My loop landed perfectly around that bull's head and shoulders. I jerked my slack and the fight was on! That bull was blowing hard and doing his best to leave. Fortunately I was able to get him dallied off on my saddle horn and stopped.

David was hollering "Nice job!"

Next we had to figure out how to get him out of there. It was not the safest place to be. I told everyone there that I was going to get behind the bull and see if he'd head back across the big ditch. The bull took off in the right direction and I followed him, keeping my dogs by my horse until I could get that bull lined out and in a safer area.

To get back to where the trailer was we had something like four electric fences to get through and one creek to cross. We were riding along and everything was going good until we got to the creek. I asked Julie to cross the creek and see what it was like. She started across but it got bad. Her horse got hung on the opposite bank because it caved in when she climbed it. The bull was really fighting me now because he wanted to go somewhere and I don't think he even cared where as long as he was moving! So I let him go into the creek but then he decided he wanted to go down the creek. David was back behind me so he cut in beside the bull and with the help of his dog kept him from taking off down the creek. I started looking for a place to climb up the opposite bank, preferably not where Julie was since her horse was still fighting to get up the bank!

Fortunately I happened to be in a better area to climb the bank. Once I climbed out I got the bull's head turned and the dogs went to work on the bull, bringing him up the bank behind me. Julie's horse finally made it out and we started moving the bull again. He was fighting to go somewhere and I liked that because we could move quickly towards the trailer. The son was running along opening gates for us and Phil, who happened to be on a four-wheeler, was following behind us by this time. We made it to the field where the truck and trailer were and I asked David to take some pictures and video for me.

Of course the bull didn't want anything to do with the trailer. I got him around to one side of the trailer and let the dogs work on him a little then I told the guy holding the trailer gate open to get ready, I was going to bring him around and I thought he'd go right into the trailer. Someone just needed to be ready to close the gate fast!

When the bull got around to the back of the trailer and saw the opening he ran right in! The guy by the gate slammed it shut.

I was sure happy to have that fight over and so was my horse. The son was happy to have the bull in the trailer so he could take him home.

Once we got the bull unloaded back at the ranch the son asked me if I would like to gather the cattle in the field behind the house. He needed to sort out this other bull away from the cows and put them in separate pens. David, Julie and I got back on our horses, took our dogs with us and headed into that back field. We ended up getting the bull sorted out from the cows and everyone in their proper pens. It only took maybe ten minutes.

When all the cattle gathering was finished for the day, David and Julie loaded up their horses and dog, said their goodbyes and left. I stayed and talked for awhile about dogs and horses then looked at some cattle the son had for sale.

I was getting ready to leave and we were walking to my truck when I saw a bull cruising down the driveway.

"Is that the bull we just sorted off the cattle in that back field behind the house?"

"Yep, it sure is!" The son said. We both stood there for a minute watching him, "You must of forgot to latch something and that bull got it open and got out!"

We tried to move him back around the house to the pen he belonged in but he just went right through the barbed wire fence and back in with the cows.

"Aw…just leave him be Marvin. He'll be another bull for another day!" So I loaded up my horse and dogs and headed back home to Oregon.

Chapter 55
Do As I Say, Not as I Do
October 2011

I got a call the other day to gather about 25 head of steers and heifers, each of them probably weighing in at 1000 pounds or more.

I called my friend Rick and asked him to come along. I brought my two best dogs, Tyson and Hangin' Tree Trap. Hangin' Tree Trap was a young dog that needed some training and I thought this would be a great opportunity to do just that. I even brought an extra horse for Rick to ride. I also told him to bring his dog Maggie because I knew it was going to be a fight to get those steers and heifers out of the swamp and tall grass where they had gone.

When Rick showed up and we started to head out I told him, "Whatever you do, if your horse stops, '*LOOK*' to see what's ahead because it might be a deep spring!"

We had a hard time getting the cattle out of the brush. The young dog, Hangin' Tree Trap, kept circling the cattle, holding them up. Finally the dogs got the cattle stopped just as my phone rang. I saw that it was someone I really needed to talk to so I answered and as I was talking, my horse Badger stopped. Not thinking about what I was doing I bumped him with my heels. My horse, being the well-broke horse he was, obeyed my command and went forward. Unfortunately he went forward into a spring and immediately sank to his belly in bog water! When his chin hit the ground I rolled off to one side but sure as heck I held my phone way up in the air and out of that water! Phones cost a lot of money!

I got my horse out of the mud, stepped up in the saddle and went to catch up with Rick. He was sitting on his horse on top of a hill laughing like crazy. I asked him if he saw what happened. "Yeah," he said with a grin, "and I sure wish I had my camera with me."

I had to tell him I was sure glad he didn't that day!

Chapter 56
The Day I Was Bit By My Own Dog
Fall 2011

I got home one evening after a long hard day of building fence. It was almost dark and I was pretty darn tired. I went into the house, kicked back in the recliner and shut my eyes so I could take a little cat nap. I was hoping I could get a few minutes of shut-eye in while my wife, Jodi, was out doing chores. After what seemed like only a minute or two, Jodi stomped into the house and said, "I can't get the goats back in the barn."

Our goats were in this half-acre turn out that we also used as an area for the dogs to exercise and play. During the day when the dogs weren't out we put our goats out there. In order for the dogs to go back out in the evening we had to round up the goats and get them in the barn. There was no way we could turn dogs and goats out together. Our dogs would just eat those poor things alive if we put them out together.

I was aggravated because I was just starting to doze off into that real relaxed kind of sleep and it was feeling pretty good. "All right" I grumbled as I hauled myself out of my chair and went out to the dog pens.

I had five or six dogs out there and three or four that would quickly and easily get the goats back in the barn for me. But since I was a bit tired and not thinking clearly I grabbed the first dog I came to which happened to be Spider. She was a little Kelpie and about the toughest dog I had. As I was leaving the kennels I also grabbed one of the sorting sticks I used to sort cattle then Spider and I walked to the turn out area.

I could just barely see the goats in the dim lighting. They were about a hundred yards away so I hissed "Get 'em" to Spider. Jodi happened to be standing on the other side of this area where she couldn't quite see me but she could sure hear me. As soon as I hissed out my command to Spider she turned and bit me on the calf! I hit her with my sorting stick and got her off my leg. In the next second she was on my leg again like she was going to eat it! Fortunately I was wearing my muck boots which were tall and reasonably tough. I hollered over to my wife, "Spider bit me!" I could hear her laughing; she must have thought getting bit by Spider was pretty funny.

I was standing there wondering why my dog bit me; that just doesn't happen. I gave her the command to get on the goats again and that son of a gun bites my leg again! I kicked her off this time then hollered over to my wife for the second time, "Geeze, she bit me again." I heard Jodi laughing.

I was thinking something was seriously wrong with this dog! My dogs didn't bite me! This dog was only a foot and a half tall and I'm six foot four. I know she didn't want to mess with me! It dawned on me that maybe she couldn't see the goats and that made me think back to the story of this old boy holding his dog up over the tall grass so she could see the cows. I was thinking, 'no', I wasn't going hold my dog up. That was just crazy! Instead I walked closer to where the goats were and all of a sudden Spider's head goes up high and her ears prick up. I could tell that she finally saw those goats. I whistled and told her to "Get 'em" and like a flash, she was gone! In a matter of seconds the goats started running to the barn and there was goat hair and feet flying everywhere. I got them caught and put in the corral, put Spider back in her kennel, went inside the house, and thankfully sat back down in my recliner.

I started thinking about what just happened and decided to call the guy who sold me Spider. When he picked up I said, "Eddie that darn dog bit me!"

He started laughing and said "What dog?"

"Spider!"

"Why'd she bite you?"

"Well, I had some goats I wanted her to bring in and to make a long story short, I hissed her on the goats and she bit me."

There was a pause then he asked "could she see them"?

"You know, I don't think so."

Now he was really laughing and said, "Let me tell you something. That dog is minding you. When she can't see those goats and you hiss at her to get them, well if you're all she can see, you're going to get bit!"

"Ah, I'm guessing that's what happened! Thanks bud, I appreciate it." We chatted a little bit more then said our goodbyes. By the time I hung up with Eddie, I could see his point and I thought it was pretty funny too.

I learned something new that day. If you had a well-trained cow dog and you were going to send them out to "Get 'em", make sure they could see whatever *"them"* was so they had something to bite besides you!

Chapter 57
Catching Cattle in Eastern Oregon
Fall 2011

I received a call from my friend Bill one evening. He had some cattle in Eastern Oregon he needed caught and hauled back over the mountain to Newberg. Unfortunately they had gotten out of their pasture and were roaming around on about 3000 acres.

I had helped haul some of these cattle over to his place the year before. Unfortunately I had worked them many times before and knew they were just plain mean and wild cattle, mostly because they were rodeo bucking stock. They didn't care what was in their way. They would kill a dog; stick a horse with a horn or whatever it took just to get away. So I thought it sounded like a fun trip!

I called my buddy Wiley and asked him to come along. I told him I would take my little gray horse Squirt for him and Badger for myself. I also planned on taking Tyson and Trap as my dog power.

The next day I met up with Wiley and we headed east. Wiley followed me in his own truck and trailer so we would be able to get the cattle over to the west side in one load. When we arrived at Bill's place we were told the cattle had thankfully come back to the ranch where they belonged. His place was only about 100 acres instead of 3000! Bill and his help had set up some panels to cover the hole where they thought the cattle escaped from earlier. Now we just needed to gather them up and load them into trailers but it wasn't really a good set up for gathering bucking stock. The pen was in the wrong spot and since these cattle had torn down fences all their lives I knew this wasn't going to be an easy situation.

We decided to take a feed truck out and see if we could get them to follow it back to the corral and get them gated in. This would be great if it worked. Unfortunately, when we tried that only six or eight head went in the corral; the rest wouldn't come near it. The only thing I could think of was to use the dogs to get the cattle in the corral. The worst thing was if these cattle got near a fence they would just tear it down and leave, especially if they felt too much pressure from the dogs. We decided to give it a try anyway because we didn't have too many other options.

We saddled our horses and got the dogs out of the truck. Wiley and I rode out and soon enough he asked me what kind of plan I had. I said, "I don't know. I think we'll just go around and try to get them through that gate down at the end of the field then into the corral."

The moment these cattle saw us coming toward them with horses and dogs they wanted no part of being caught; they were ready to "leave the country"! I sent the dogs out with the command "Get 'em". Right away the dogs bayed up the cattle in the middle of the field we were in and held them there. I turned to Wiley and said, "Man Wiley, we could do anything with them in a field this big but as soon as we get them near a fence they're just going to tear it down and leave."

Well that was the chance we'd have to take if we were going to get them into the corral. So we carefully tried to move them down the fence line toward the gate but sure enough they took off and ran. I sent the dogs out and got them stopped again. Again we started toward the cattle nice and slow hoping to just gently push them through the gate and into the corral but they took one look at us coming at them and bolted. There was one old black cow in the herd and I was told she was the worst on the fences. Little did I know there was a weak spot in the fence where they had torn it down the week before and someone had done a quick patch. That old black cow tore through the fence at that weak spot and all the calves and bulls followed her. They all got through the fence and out onto the 3000 acres. I sent Tyson and Trap to stop them. I wasn't able to follow because there was one strand of barbed wire that didn't break and I didn't want my horse to get caught stepping over it.

I heard Trap barking and knew he had the cattle bayed up. I told Wiley I was going to cut the fence and ride out there to help my dogs. After I cut the wire I rode out to where I could get on the backside of the cows then I called the dogs back there with me.

Luckily for us the cows headed back to the property right through the hole in the fence where they had escaped! However, that old black cow had to go down a little further and tear out a whole new section of fence to get back into the field! She just liked tearing up fence! I told Wiley we needed to try and get them stopped in the middle of the field again. I sent the dogs out there to stop them. Of course there were a couple of cows that went back through the fence onto the 3000 acres. I got the dogs to stop the ones that stayed in the field. They were strung out for about a 100 yards by then and were going in all directions. I rode out there and didn't even know where to start. I told Wiley we needed to get them all balled up and that was an understatement!

We started working the cows with the dogs and horses and we finally got them back in a ball. We tried to move them toward the corral and they took off again. For the second time they tore the fence down. They were back on the 3000 acres. *'Geeze,'* I'm thinking. *'What a mess!'*

I sent the dogs out to stop them. I rode back to the first hole I had opened and went through it onto the 3000 acres after the cattle. I managed to get them headed back to Bill's property when they jumped the fence this time and took off in about ten different directions across the field! I said, "Wiley, We've got to get them stopped." With the help of the dogs we once again got them stopped and bayed up close to a corner of the fence. They just stood there. I think they might have finally had enough of my dogs and all that running! Those cattle were smart though. They had known my dogs for years and they'd been chewed on before so they learned not to run away. But they only learned not to run away if I could get them in one small herd. If they split up they knew the dogs couldn't keep up with forty cows heading twenty directions!

We got them held up but by then this chase and fight had been going on for over an hour. My dogs were tired, my horse was tired and I was tired! I called Bill on the cell phone. I wanted to find out where he was. When he answered he told me he was four or five hundred yards away over by the corral. I told him over the phone, "Bill, I don't know man. I think I'm going to make one more try and if I can't get them I'm done. I'm giving up. We've all had enough; we've torn down enough fences for one day."

"Marvin, you can get them in here, I know you can. You always have!"

"I know but this is different man. Everything is just not set up to win. It's set up to lose and I don't like losing. I think we need to quit and re-group."

"No man." Bill pleaded. His son Billy was there and I could hear him in the background, "You can get them in Marvin I know you can."

"Okay!" I said with some resignation, "We'll take one more stab at it. If I can get everybody to do exactly what I tell them, go where I say and don't move anywhere I don't say to, we might have a chance. We'll try to bring them right across the middle of that field. I think I can hold them together down the center. It's when they get near a fence I can't hold them and they tear it down. The dogs can't hold them when they're going ten different directions either."

Everyone agreed to do what I asked so I summoned up the last of my energy and said, "Let's give it one more try!"

We ended up moving the cows across the middle of the field. This time we got them across it successfully by going right down the middle! Every time a cow tried to move out of the bunch I got a dog on them and they went right back into the ball. It probably took 20 minutes to take them 200 feet! I only wanted them to walk. In fact, at this point, I'd rather they balled up and not move at all than try to take off at a trot. We finally got them over to the side fence and I was going to lead them into the corral. I hollered for Bill's son. He stuck his head around the corner. He was hiding behind a tree by the corral so as not to disrupt the cattle from going into the corral! He whispered loudly, "Marvin, I'm right here."

"Don't move!" I told him, "your perfect right there." I then quietly said to Wiley, "Can you just keep riding up the side? I'm going to move my horse toward the cattle a couple of steps." I wanted both Wiley and Trap to help hold the side.

Tyson and Trap were on a roll. I moved those dogs two inches at a time that day. They were tired of working these cattle so they listened to me really well; I think they wanted these cattle in the corral as much as we did!

We started moving the cattle an inch at a time. I looked over at Wiley riding my horse Squirt and working these bucking stock cattle with me. I thought it was fun that he was getting a chance to do some crazy stuff like this with me! We kept those cattle slowly moving, sometimes they'd only move a foot and then they would stop. When they would stop I'd get a dog up by a cow and I'd have that dog walk up six inches and that cow would walk around the herd to the cow in front of it. Then I'd do this for another cow. Sometimes the whole herd would shuffle forward a little bit. This method was literally a matter of moving one cow at a time to get them closer to the corral.

I was moving Badger sometimes one step at a time. That's all the speed we could make because I just didn't want to lose them again. As long as they were headed toward the corral and they were just walking we were good. I kept having Trap move them up a foot or two at a time. Then another calf would move forward. I would have the dogs stop and lay down when the herd moved too much. Then I would ask Tyson to creep up. Wiley was moving Squirt only a step or two at a time also. I bet it took 30 minutes of this dance to only go 100 feet!

Finally we got all the cattle in the corral, ran up, slammed the gate and got it chained up.

At that moment Bill came around the corner with a tractor. He put it right up against the two panels we had just shut. "What are you doing," I asked.

"I figured they're going to try to tear these panels down." The corral was made up of six foot panels. There weren't any gates. "They know where they came in and I'm sure they'll try to ram the panels to get out the same way they did before!"

"Okay…." I agreed then suggested, "How about we try to get them loaded before they tear out of there?"

We had three trailers with us on the property to load cattle in. Wiley backed his big trailer up to the panels. Just as he was backing up the cattle started hitting the two panels where Bill had put the tractor! They were actually trying to tear it down, just like Bill said.

"Man alive!" I exclaimed as I watched them batter against the tractor, "Let's get them in the trailers before they smash that tractor apart and end up back out in the brush!"

We loaded Wiley's trailer and moved it off to the side then got the rest of the cattle in Bill's trailer. Since we were able to fit them all in two trailers, I didn't need to haul any which made me happy because I was hauling my horses and dogs anyhow. Once the cattle were all loaded up and secure, I took my dogs to a nearby pond so they could cool off.

Wiley and I told Bill we'd see him on the other side of the mountain with his cattle, I loaded up the dogs and horses in my trailer and we caravanned back across the mountain. We all stopped and ate dinner on our way home and by the time we got across Mt. Hood it was just getting dark. When Wiley and I arrived at Bill's property on this side of the mountain I said, "Wiley, those cattle aren't going to be here in the morning. They're going to tear a fence down tonight and leave."

"You think so?"

"Yeah, I know so! They're not going to stay here because we're unloading them in the dark. I know these cattle."

We unloaded the cattle then everyone got into their rigs and headed home.

The next morning I went back to where we'd unloaded the cattle to do some fence work on a neighboring property. As I was taking my tractor off the flatbed trailer I looked around. There was not a cow to be seen!

Chapter 58
A Rodeo Steer In The Christmas Trees
Fall 2011

Wiley called me one day about catching a steer. He had leased out several steers to a Mexican rodeo in Canby a while back and had gone to pick them up. Right away he said, "Man, I went to get my roping steers back from the Mexican rodeo people and one of them was gone. He jumped the fence and they couldn't catch him. I wanted to know if you would help me catch him?"

"Sure." I was always up for catching troublesome cattle!

"The steer is somewhere on 20 acres of overgrown Christmas trees by the rodeo grounds."

"That's no problem. We'll get him!"

"Bring your horse and dogs."

"Do I need to bring two horses," I asked Wiley before hanging up.

"No I'm going to have to be on foot to help find him and push him out of the brush."

The next morning I hooked up my trailer since I had to haul my horse and a steer. I took my dogs Tyson and Trap and my horse Badger. Next I drove over to Wiley's Lone Star ranch and picked him up and we headed to Canby to catch the missing roping steer.

When Wiley got in the truck I asked him, "What does he weigh?"

"I don't know, probably 700 pounds and he has big ol' horns too!

We arrived at the pasture in Canby, unloaded everyone, and headed in. Wiley said he'd probably be back in the overgrown Christmas trees. These trees were 30 or 40 feet tall, a bit bigger than your average Christmas tree size. The bad thing about our situation was all the cross-fencing throughout the pasture. It looked somewhat challenging but I figured we might as well get started, "All right let's go see if we can find him." I told Wiley.

On this particular day it was raining and miserable. I didn't have my slickers or any other rain gear with me so I knew I was going to get wet and probably cold too if it took a long time. With Wiley on foot and me on Badger we set out to look for the steer.

I rode out with Tyson and Trap to a little clearing where there were Christmas trees on both sides of me. Trap went one way and Tyson went another. Tyson was pretty good at tracking cattle but in a situation like this I liked having Trap because he barked when he had something bayed up and then I knew he'd found whatever I sent him to get.

I never heard Trap bark but soon enough I heard Wiley shout, "Tyson found him."

I hollered at Tyson to "Bring him" and about that time Tyson barked a little. Trap took off to find Tyson because he knew if Tyson was barking he had cattle! Trap and Tyson were working together to bring this steer out of the trees when he dodged to the side and started going the wrong way! I saw the steer cross the area where I was sitting on Badger. He was about 60 feet from me. I wasn't able to get to him in time to throw a rope on him and he took off into the Christmas trees on the far side! I loped Badger toward the trees but had to stop. There was one strand of barbed wire about four feet off the ground so I couldn't get into the Christmas trees. I was hollering at the dogs to get ahead and get the steer stopped.

They finally stopped him and I went around the other side of the Christmas trees. Before I got there the steer took off again and the dogs went after him fighting him along the way. Wiley hollered, "He's back down here!" I went back around the trees and got on the other side of the little barbed wire fence. The steer went across the clearing again and back into the other side of the Christmas trees where he had been when we first started this! Man alive, I felt like a yo-yo! I told the dogs to "Bring 'em". They brought him back out and he got within 50 feet of me again but I still wasn't able to throw a rope on him. He ran back under the single strand of barbed wire again and I wasn't able to go after him. I went back around to the other side to see if I could get him that way. Then I saw that the dogs had him bayed up by the arena! I rode toward where they had him stopped but could only get about 30 feet from him and not any closer. Every time I tried he would try to run over my dogs and leave.

There was this one tree limb between me and the steer which prevented me from throwing a rope on him. I moved my horse forward another three feet. I had my reins, all my coils, and my rope in my left hand. I also had to grab the tree branch with my left hand and pull it back so I could throw a rope on the steer with my right hand. I swung the loop by my side and got it on one of the steer's horns but he threw it off before I could get it on both horns. I did this about three times. On the fourth time I threw it around his left horn but couldn't get it around his right horn because of the way he was standing. Tyson was over on the steers left side. I told Tyson to step up a little bit and when he did that steer turned his head at Tyson and I jerked my slack and got my loop tight. Just as I pulled that loop tight the steer took off and went around the side of my horse and around a tree. I moved my horse forward to get in line with the steer but my horse stopped and wouldn't move.

I have learned that if my horse won't move then there was probably something wrong. I dallied the steer on my saddle horn but by then he had about 40 feet of rope out. I told my dogs to lie down. I looked down the side of my horse and saw that he was standing in a bunch of old barbed wire that was lying on the ground. He was all tangled up in it. I instantly let my rope go and threw it off the saddle horn then told the dogs to get ahead. I hollered at Wiley, "Hey…Badger's caught up in barbed wire. I'm going to cut my horse out then I'll take after that steer again." The steer had 60 feet of ranch rope trailing out behind him and he was dragging it all around in the mud! But I had other things to worry about at the moment. I stepped down from the saddle and pulled out my Leatherman's tool to cut off the barbed wire. Then I had to move all the wire so I could get my horse out of there. When I was finally able to safely lead Badger out of that spot, I hollered at Wiley, "Hey man, where's the steer?"

Wiley pointed out that the dogs had him back down by the side of the arena. I said, "All right I'm going to go around to the other side." I tried to come up on the lower side so I could get my rope picked up. Of course the steer took off before I could pick the rope up and the dogs ran after him fighting him to stop. Wiley yelled toward me, "Hey Marvin, that steer ran into the arena!" I loped Badger around to the other end so I could reach the gate. There happened to be a little four foot gate that was open and the steer had run through it and into the arena. The dogs had him bayed up back in the lane that went to the stripping chute.

"Let's just bring him down that lane and put him in the stripping chute and bring him out that side." I suggested to Wiley when he caught up to me. The dogs brought him all the way around to the stripping chute. They even actually got him up in the chute!

"What now?" Wiley asked me.

"I'm just going to ride out into the arena." The mud was about six inches deep in this arena and it was a real mess. "You can hand me that rope dragging off of him. I'll coil it up and dally him off. You open the gate and we'll head for the trailer."

The trailer was sitting down in the middle of the field. Wiley handed me the end of that muddy rope and I coiled it up, got it dallied off to the saddle horn then told him to open the gate. When he opened the gate that steer just moseyed out in the arena. I rode across the arena with the dogs bringing the steer up behind me! We got him back out the other end of the arena and headed for the trailer. Once we got down there I just held him until Wiley caught up since he was on foot. We opened the trailer gate but the steer slipped over to the side and I had to have the dogs fight with him a little bit to bring him back around. After that little bit of dog action the steer jumped right into the trailer as fast as he could! He was done with this dog fighting stuff! I slammed the trailer gate then we pushed him up in the front so I could close the divider and load my horse in the back. I petted the dogs for a little while before loading them up in the truck.

Wiley said, "That was just too much fun."

"Yeah I guess so…other than the six inches of mud, the rain and the barbed wire!"

We headed back to Wiley's place. When I pulled up somebody asked me if I caught the steer. "Yeah!" I said then added, "He's in the trailer and he's happy to be there!"

I unloaded that steer into Wiley's arena, back with the rest of the steers. He must have enjoyed his experience in the Christmas trees because he got into the habit of jumping fences which forced Wiley to finally sell him!

Chapter 59
The Cow Who Hit The House
Winter 2011

One winter I was asked to catch a herd of these tough, ornery cattle in Eastern Oregon and bring them back to the west side for a guy I knew named Bill. It was dark when I arrived on Bill's property with the herd and we had no choice but to unload them at night into his field. The next day I happened to be over at his place moving some equipment when I noticed there weren't any cattle in his field. I knew for a fact that there had been 44 head in there the night before!

This of course was a problem. I was then asked to help find Bill's cattle! So I called a friend of mine, Wiley, to see if he wanted to help. I knew he'd jump at the opportunity since he'd never been on a cattle seeking and gathering expedition like this before! I figured I'd take my two horses; Squirt as the spare for Wiley along with my trusty mount, Badger. I also choose Tyson and Trap as my dog power. At the last minute I decided to call Rick, another buddy of mine, to see if he wanted to help. Nobody had any clue where these cattle went. I was guessing they were up on the mountain on Bill's property somewhere so the more help out there looking, the better.

Rick decided to bring his dog Maggie along which was fine with me. Maggie is actually from a litter out of my Tyson dog so I knew the kind of cattle ability she was bringing to the table!

Wiley, Rick and I met at the property where Bill and some of his neighbors were gathered. I asked if anybody had any idea where the cattle might be. The guy who lived next door to Bill said he thought they were up on the mountain since he saw them there yesterday.

So we all set off toward that mountain looking for those cows but after a while it became apparent we weren't having any luck. Wiley and I happened to be riding horses but Rick was on foot since he didn't have a horse at the time. The plan was for him to wait at the bottom of the mountain and for us to ride up it. We figured we'd stay in communication with our two-way radios but quickly discovered that two of the radios worked and two didn't which meant I and the guy on the four-wheeler who was helping out could keep in touch but me, Rick and Wiley couldn't if we split up.

Wiley and I rode higher and higher up that mountain searching for the cattle. We rode and rode and never saw anything remotely looking like a cow. Bill's neighbor who was on the four-wheeler helping us look for the cattle rode over to us one of the times our paths crossed and we stopped to catch up and compare notes on our progress. He hadn't seen any cows so far. I told him the only thing we saw were some tracks and I thought they were heading east. I figured on following those tracks out. That was fine with him. He told us in parting, "I'll go the other way."

Wiley and I rode all the way up to Bald Peak Road which was high on the mountain top and we were still only following cattle tracks! About that time the guy on the four-wheeler called us on the radio that worked and said he spotted the cattle. They were back where we had been an hour ago and heading down the mountain!

We took off with our horses, going through blackberries, trees and brush. The guy on the four-wheeler caught up to us once we were mostly down the mountain side. I asked him, "Where'd they go?"

"I don't know now!" He said, "The last I saw them they were headed down this mountain."

"Well, we'll ride on down to the bottom and see if we can find them there." Wiley and I kept our horses headed down. We finally ended up at the bottom of the mountain and rode out into a field. I glanced to my right and suddenly saw the cattle coming right at us! And of course these are the type of cattle that aren't scared of anything. I mean they'll run through you, over you, by you; whatever they felt like doing!

I sent Tyson and Trap, who'd been diligently trotting alongside of me this whole time, to get ahead of these cattle and get them stopped. They ran towards that big herd and it was almost comical because nobody would think they had any kind of chance stopping them. Those two dogs together might weigh 115 pounds and there were at least 40 head in this herd. But, amazingly, all those cattle stopped dead in their tracks. And as quick as they stopped, they turned the other way and took off!

The cattle went running down this nearby gravel road bordering some pastures but they were headed the wrong way so I sent the dogs to get ahead of them. Tyson ran to the head cow and tried to stop it. My dog Trap gets an attitude sometimes with cattle. If any cow charges at him while he's working them, he'll stop to fight. Unfortunately I haven't been able to train him enough to get him out of this habit. Trap got about half way around the herd when this old cow blows out at him. She stomped and charged at him fully intending to do her best to kill him. Trap launched himself at her head, locked onto it and started biting on her. Then Tyson decided to shoot back from his position at the front of the herd to help Trap out. I needed to stop this so I could keep the herd moving smoothly so I hollered at them to get off that cow and get to the head. The cattle were pretty strung out down this gravel road by then and some were even in this other guy's field. By this time it was just me and my two dogs. I had managed to lose Wiley and Rick somewhere along the way! One minute they were right behind me and the next minute they were nowhere to be seen.

When I got the dogs off that one cow and focused back on the herd, they finally managed to get all the cattle stopped. I was just sitting there trying to figure out how to get them back to where I wanted them to go. I gave the dogs the command to "Bring 'em" in order to turn them and bring them toward me. Then I rode down the road a ways to block them from going that way. Well the herd came out across the gravel road but then headed back up the mountain where they came from! Rick and Wiley still hadn't shown up to help and I wasn't sure how all this was going to work out with just me and the dogs! I started hollering at Tyson and Trap to "Come by", the command for tracking around the left side of the cattle and moving them. Within a few minutes they got the herd turned and headed back towards the property where they belonged except for one straggler cow that wouldn't stay with the herd. About that time Rick showed up on foot with Maggie.

I said to him, "Rick keep an eye on this straggler cow, I m going to cut this herd off and get them headed back to that gate in the corner of the field where they belong." The dogs and I were going around the side of the herd when I saw two calves cut out and head for the mountains. I decided to just let those two go at the moment. The dogs and I managed to get the cattle turned into the pasture. I was assuming they were all accounted for except the two calves that got away and the one straggler cow Rick was keeping an eye on. But then Rick walked up with Maggie and I asked, "Where did the straggler cow go?"

"She cut back in through the woods. I'm guessing she went back in with the herd."

"Well, never mind about her. We lost two calves up on the side of this mountain. Let's try to find them!"

We got the pasture gate shut on the main group of cattle and then I told the guy on the four-wheeler to concentrate on the two that went up the hill. "We'll see if we can find them." Wiley showed up by this time on his horse and soon everybody was looking for these two calves.

After a little bit of riding we found them and had the dogs bay them up in the brush. Since Wiley team ropes and I ranch rope I said, "Let's try to move these two out of here and get them out in that field and see if we can't rope them." We started moving them with the horses but they split up on us. One went one way and one went another way. I had Tyson and Trap with me so I sent them both to get the one closest to me bayed up but it ended up in the blackberries and I couldn't get to it. Then I heard Rick and Wiley a little ways off hollering and carrying on.

I was sitting there just watching this one calf I had bayed up in the blackberries when I thought to myself, *Well shoot, I might as well try to get a rope on her'.* I could still hear Wiley and Rick making a heck of a lot of noise so I assumed they had that other calf roped, bayed up with Maggie or something like that. I attempted to rope this one big calf but finally ended up losing her. I just couldn't get to her with the rope through all the black-berries and finally she ran off. I figured I should probably go find Rick and Wiley at this point. I started riding down the mountain side when I ran into Wiley riding up it.

I asked "Where did your calf go?

He said, "I don't know man. It was going down across the road and Rick was after her with his dog. His dog was fighting her but she wouldn't stop."

"So where is it?" I asked again.

"I don't know. It's across the road and down through that field some-where. Rick is still on it with his dog."

"Well let's ride down there and see." So we both rode down that way. Pretty soon we met up with Rick and his dog walking towards us.

"Where's that calf?" I asked Rick.

"She's down there in that guy's corral but watch out 'cuz she is mean! I had Maggie chewing on her head pretty good and she didn't even slow down. She went through that barbed wire fence over there." Rick pointed to a busted up fence.

"Well let's ride down there and see if we can get her roped." I mo-tioned for Wiley to follow me and my horse down the hill while Rick walked down an old gravel road alongside this guy's fence. Soon enough the guy whose fence it was pulled up on a four-wheeler.

"Where're you all going" he said in a tough sounding voice.

I politely told him, "Were going down there to try to get that big ol' calf out of that corral of yours."

"I don't have a calf in my corral." He stated in a very no-nonsense way.

"You do now!"

"I'm telling you I don't!"

"Well sir, I can see her from right here! She's red and white and she's got a bit of blood on her head! She's standing down there in your corral."

"Who does she belong to?"

"She belongs to a guy named Bill."

"Bill?" the guy asked. "He's not supposed to have cattle up here. He moved them out of here."

"Well they moved back. They were across the road until they all got out. Honestly, all we'd like to do is get her out of your corral."

"I'm telling you she isn't there."

"Sir, she's in there. I see her from right here."

He walked a little down his drive and was finally able to see her. He turned back to me and said, "Okay then. I'll go run her out this gate and down this back road and you can do whatever you want with her!"

"Well I don't recommend you try running this calf anywhere 'cause she's mean. I'm telling you, she'll hurt you." By then he'd already walked down the driveway ignoring me. We rode our horses a little ways behind him with Rick following along on foot. Soon enough I hollered out to the guy, "She's out there and I can see her plain as day! She's just snot blowing mean looking."

He turned around real quick and told us, "I'll just go out there and you guys wait here and I'll run her out to you."

Again I emphatically told him, "Sir I wouldn't go out there!" He ignored me again and took about three steps toward that calf before she turned and took about five menacing steps toward him! She probably weighed 1200 pounds, was mean to begin with and now was just plain angry.

The guy hesitated a moment, thought better about taking any more steps toward her, then asked me, "Well, what do you plan on doing?"

"I think we'll just go out there and I'll try to get her to come out that hole in your fence, then out this gate then I'll put a rope on her."

That was an agreeable plan to the guy so I started walking my horse toward the cow and she started walking toward me. I said to the guy, "You know, she's probably going to bust some boards in the fence. I'll come back later to put your three boards up...or we'll just buy you new ones."

In a very gruff manner he told me, "I don't care what you do, I want her off my property!"

"Sir," I looked him straight in the eye, "You don't want her off your property nearly as bad as I do!"

I kept heading toward her on Badger when she made a sudden charge at me then quickly turned and raced off the other way. Now she was running toward the board fence like I wanted her too. There were three boards already torn off this fence. The cow went through that spot then tore across the field on the other side so I set my dogs on her. The cow, with both dogs on her, raced into an area of overgrown, brushy filberts where my dogs got her bayed up. Wiley and I rode down there so we could rope her. It just so happened that there was a gal there with a camera to capture some of this action and we ended up with some pretty cool pictures.

Rick's dog, Maggie, hadn't had much training in fighting cattle like this where my dogs, Tyson and Trap, knew the ropes! I could tell them to "Bite", "Back off", and "Lay down"; they would do whatever I commanded. Rick's dog Maggie was getting mad because she'd been fighting this cow for a while now. I told my dogs to back off and lay down when this cow stopped so I could try to ride up and put a rope on her. Before I could get my rope on her, here came Maggie. She ran in and grabbed a hold of this cow's nose and the fight was on. Of course my dogs, not wanting to miss out on this action, jumped in the middle of it. I started yelling at Rick to get his dog out of there which he finally did, I called off my dogs, and I was now able to get a rope on the cow.

Once I had her roped I pulled her out in the field. Wiley tried to rope her hind feet but he kept missing because she was running every which way. Finally I just started pulling her across this field toward the gate that was four or five hundred feet away. I had her almost there before I choked her down so she laid down. Rick caught up with me by this time. I could tell the property owner was mad as a hornet; seemed he was just ticked off about everything.

"Rick, walk up there and ask that guy if we can bring the truck and trailer down here and back it up to the gate. I'll take this cow over there with my horse and we'll put her in my trailer."

Rick walked over to the guy and talked to him for a minute or two then came back to me, "He said we could do it." I was pretty relieved at that! Rick walked back to get the truck and trailer.

I got this cow up and walked over near the gate, then choked her down a little bit. She was just standing there blowing, snot mad. Rick came down the road with the truck and trailer. He backed it up to the gate. "All right," I said, "everybody get ready." Someone opened the trailer gate. "I'm going to let her get up then sic my dogs on her. Everybody stay out of the way 'cause I think she's going to want to go in that trailer!" Everybody stepped back a ways. Rick, who had gotten out of the truck, went over and ducked behind the trailer gate. I loosened the rope on the cow then set Tyson and Trap on her. It was like an instant explosion of dogs and cow; the cow was swinging her head and thrashing at the dogs and there was a lot of barking and snarling going on. Within a minute that cow turned from the dogs, raced by me and my horse and ran right into the trailer. Rick slammed the trailer gate shut and exclaimed, "Man, that was all right!"

"Yeah that worked pretty well! Let's get her shut up in the front part of this trailer. Then we'll put her back in the right field!"

Rick drove her back up the road. Wiley and I rode our horses back to the pasture at a nice, slow walk, letting them cool off. I was thinking we were totally done with the cattle gathering, at least that was what I was hoping. But no, there was still a calf missing and we needed to find it!

We rode up to Rick and the pasture where the rest of the herd was and I said to him," What about that one straggler cow that got away Rick?"

I happened to have a guy there who was working on fixing the fence that got torn up by these cows the night before. He overheard me asking Rick about the cow and hollered over to me, "Marvin, there's a cow down here in the woods."

I'm thinking *'Oh Man, not a good spot to be.'* He told me she was between the fence and the road.

I turned to Wiley and Rick, "Let's go get her guys. While we're all here we might as well get her." I asked the guy fixing the fence, "Can you run her out of there?"

"Yeah, maybe." He sounded a bit hesitant but went tromping off into the woods anyway. We headed down to the edge of the woods near the fence and got ready. Pretty soon the cow came flying out and shot up the road. You could tell this fence guy had never seen anything like that before.

I hollered to Wiley, "Man, let's go get her." We spurred our horses into a gallop. I could see her just hauling up this gravel road like she was headed for the center of town! I wasn't about to run my horse that hard on the gravel road just to get this cow stopped, so I called for Tyson and Trap to get ahead of her. They ran out fast and soon I saw them pass her going up this hill. Then I watched her turn up this driveway with the dogs on her heels. I was hoping that the cow would get blocked up at the top of that driveway and turn around to come back down it. That meant she had to come by me to get out and I was planning on roping her. Well the cow went up that driveway but she didn't come back down! So I trotted my horse up the driveway to see what was going on.

Strangely enough I didn't see my dogs and I didn't see the cow. I didn't see anything but a house and a fence. I rode around the house when all of a sudden I saw the cow at the end of the house and she was banging her head on it! Bang, bang, bang! I could hear her loud and clear all the way from where I was. 'Oh man!' I thought. I was sitting there on my horse about 30 feet from this cow. The dogs had her bayed up right against the side of the house. Pretty soon I saw the blinds on a window open and a lady's face peer out! I'm thinking *'oh great, now I'm in trouble!'* The blinds snapped shut. I rode up to the corner of the house because the last thing I wanted was for this lady to walk out of the house and get charged by this snot-blowing mean cow.

Lucky for me I'd met this gal a few days before because I was there building fence and I had explained to her how we were going to put cows out in the field. She was a nice enough young lady. However, she worked nights and probably didn't get home until the morning so I was guessing she had just gone to bed when this cow hit the side of her house! She opened the door about six inches and stuck her head out. I automatically called out, "Sorry."

She looked at me, then over at the cow, then, after a slight pause she said loudly and very emphatically, "DO NOT RUN THAT COW INTO MY HOUSE!"

"Okay ma'am, I won't!" I quickly said. She slammed the door shut.

I was sitting there on my horse thinking this wasn't a very good situation. The cow had to go around this lady's house to get out. And the last thing I wanted to do was have this cow hit the lady's house again. I wasn't sure if she had guns or not! We all just sat there quietly for a moment. My horse cocked up his back foot in a resting position; my dogs laid quietly on the ground and the cow was being good and just standing there.

When you get in these situations the best thing to do is take a five minute break and think things through. What the heck was I going do now? I spotted Wiley and Rick at the end of the driveway so I hollered to them, "Can you guys open that fence down there?" We had a bunch of cattle panels we put up to form a temporary gate where the fence was busted. "I'm going to try and get this cow to come around the side of the house." I was really hoping that she'd see the hole in the fence and go back in.

My son, Jason, and his girl friend arrived right at that time. They came sauntering into the field as all this was going on with the cow. I had called him earlier and told him to stop by if he needed some excitement! Jason could see exactly what I was trying to do so he jumped right in and opened up one of the panels. I slowly moved my horse at the cow who started running alongside the house. I was just trying to let everything go easy. She was trotting along and I was praying she didn't hit the house. Then she zipped around the side of the house, cut down to the fence, went through the hole and back into the field where she belonged. Jason slammed the panel shut and we tied them securely back together.

"Ohhhh man! I said, "You guys don't know how lucky we are!"

"Why?" Someone uttered.

I explained what the cow did to the lady's house. Everybody started laughing and laughing. We never did find that other calf but we got the rest of those cows all caught up!